Violations:
Stories of Love by
Latin American
Women

Violations
Stories of Love by
Latin American
Women

Edited and with an introduction
by Psiche Hughes
Foreword by Brian Matthews

UNIVERSITY OF NEBRASKA PRESS

LINCOLN & LONDON

Acknowledgments for the use of
copyrighted material appear on pages
181–82, which constitute an extension
of the copyright page. Copyright ©
2004 by the Board of Regents of
the University of Nebraska. All rights
reserved. Typeset on the Macintosh
computer, using Adobe Minion fonts.
Book design by R. Eckersley. Printed
by Edwards Brothers, Inc. Manufac-
tured in the United States of America.
ⓧ

Library of Congress Cataloging-in-
Publication Data
Violations : stories of love by Latin
American women / edited and with
an introduction by Psiche Hughes ;
foreword by Brian Matthews.
p. cm. – (Latin American women
writers)
ISBN 0-8032-2418-4 (hardcover : alk.
paper) –
ISBN 0-8032-7347-9 (pbk. : alk. paper)
1. Latin American fiction – women
authors – Translations into
English.   2. Love stories, Latin American – Translations into English.
I. Hughes, Psiche. II. Series.
PQ7087.E5V565 2004
863.008'03543'082–dc22   2004004123

To my Philip,
whose ceaseless help
and faith in my project
made completion
possible.

In the art of language, one calls metaphors that which is used to convey a meaning other than its own. Therefore metaphors are the perversions of language, and perversions are the metaphors of love.

KARL KRAUS

CONTENTS

Historically, the love story has been the preserve of women writers. This was especially so in Latin America until well into the last century, a society dominated by religion that imposed moral, stylistic, and thematic constraints – a code of decency – on the fictional treatment of love and passion. The explicitly physical, the erotic, the intimacies of human sexual relationship were forbidden territory for Latin American women writers. Romantic situations delicately and sensitively portrayed represented the furthest limits available to them.

In recent years, however, all that has changed. In this collection, Psiche Hughes has brought together stories by women who are not only vigorously challenging the code of decency but who are in some cases fracturing the whole fictional convention of the love story. An authority on modern Latin American literature, especially novels and short stories, Hughes shows graphically in this collection how Latin American women writers, emerging toward the end of the twentieth century, violently challenge in their short fiction both literary conventions and legal or quasilegal proscription. These are stories in which "violation" – in the realms of both private sexual behavior and of imposed public morality – is a central concept and a central mode of action.

These stories are both shocking and exhilarating, violent and tender, familiar yet groundbreaking. Through them, Hughes demonstrates the revolutionary changes that have overtaken Latin American women's short fiction in recent years and reveals, by unerring selection, its radical individuality – the lush, "doubly baroque" style, the poetic language, the sometimes shocking juxtapositions and imagery, the obsession with psychoanalysis.

This is a rich Latin American feast of fiction by women writers who are feisty, scornful of convention, and, above all, passionate and proud of it.

Brian Matthews

ACKNOWLEDGMENTS

To select and connect the individual works of sixteen writers proved a task full of unsuspected obstacles. I am therefore very grateful to all who helped me.

My first thanks go to the authors of the stories, whose approval and enthusiasm made it possible. Some were dear friends to start with; some, excitingly, became new friends.

I owe a lot to Jane Arms in Australia, whose editing and constant encouragement were invaluable, and also to her husband, the author Brian Matthews.

Here in the UK I must thank my old friends: Beryl Bainbridge for her comments, not always flattering but always very discerning; Alicia Arendar for sorting out some tricky Spanish American terms; dear colleagues: Carole Gill and Evi Fishburne for their advice; A. Duttmann for enlightening me over a quotation from Heidegger; Dani Gutfreund for her help in Brazilian Portuguese; and Clare James who so patiently interpreted my handwriting.

Violation of the Love Story

The love story has traditionally been associated with women's fiction, especially in Latin American countries where its representation has up to the middle of the last century been confined to romantic situations delicately and sensitively portrayed. In a society dominated by Catholicism, women's sexuality had to be sanctified by marriage, when not repressed, and therefore confined to the domestic scene and procreation. Consequently, its literary expression avoided physical terminology, let alone anything that could be construed as erotic. Erotic and later pornographic language was the province of men.

More recently, however, women have broken away from this tradition and launched into more explicit and outspoken descriptions of sexual behavior, abandoning the code of "decency" originally imposed upon their literary language. Some women have even gone further, including the writers whose works figure here: by breaking with the conventional patterns they have violated the whole concept of the "love story," along with the very notion of traditional love. I am referring to violation in both its objective and subjective senses: love as victim of social restraints and love as threatening existing social and psychological structures. The stories by Latin American women presented in this collection have been selected because they are different and exciting, and they illustrate the various forms in which this violation occurs.

The concepts of transgression and violation, certainly in the tradition established by the French writer Georges Bataille (1897–1962), are linked to the Law. They are concerned with exceeding the limits or bounds prescribed by laws, whether explicit or implicit, social, religious, political or sexual. This spirit of transgression is evoked in the following texts. Accordingly, I have conceived the following classification of the texts presented here: (1) infringement of the social code; (2) infringement of the religious code; (3) indictment of historical and political structures; and (4) perversion of the sexual ethos. I hope this schematic classification will clarify the choice of texts in the present collection.

Concerning the first of these classifications, violation can operate on a purely linguistic level, as in the ironic intent of Margo Glantz's story about the English incapacity to express love in passionate terms, or in the jocular irreverence with which Alicia Steimberg describes girls' preoccupation with sex, their fantasies and other manifestations of their desire. The unsuspected situation and the deliberately pornographic language of "Young Amatista" mock any preconceived romantic ideas about the innocence of young females. In terms of the codes that control conjugal life, Ángeles Mastretta's and Marilyn Bobes's stories humorously, when not cynically, deal with the question of sexual frustration and the consequent incidence of adultery; Liliana Heker's biting satire presents a housewife obsessively preoccupied with domestic cleanliness and the uncanny consequences of such preoccupation; while marriage for Sylvia Lago's heroine is reduced to a socially recognized form of prostitution that totally destroys the woman's ethical values. Another facet of prostitution is dealt with in Luisa Valenzuela's latest story, which she has personally entrusted to me for translation and inclusion in the collection.

Concerning the infringement of the religious code, we recall how the language of love has been used and conventionally associated with religious writing in Judeo–Christian cultures to express the mystical experience, from the Song of Solomon down to the works of John of the Cross, Teresa of Ávila, et al., whereas the cult of the Virgin has been associated throughout the centuries with the language of flowers. Both of these traditions are satirized by the iconoclastic theme of Armonía Somers's story about a black man running away from the authorities, haunted by fear and hunger, finding brief comfort and refuge in the living image of the Virgin Mary.

On a political level, the love story serves as a subversive comment, be it in Carmen Boullosa's account of Montezuma's brief love affair upon returning to Mexico four centuries later to view the sequel to the Conquest, or in the parable by the Brazilian Nélida Piñon about two lovers breaking socially accepted rules of conduct for which they are imprisoned and tortured. In both, the indictment of the tyrannies and corruption in Latin America is forcefully outlined.

Finally, concerning the sexual ethos, love is humorously subverted in the story by Cristina Peri Rossi, in which sexual desire is replaced by culinary fantasies. Food – in the form of excessive eating and consequent obesity – is again connected with sexual attraction and love in Andrea Blanqué's story. In Ana María Shua's story, the theme of sexual jealousy surviving the death of love is ironically treated. Fantasizing also becomes an element of transgression in the morbid atmosphere of Fanny Buitrago's hospital ward, where the love of twelve inmates for one beautiful male patient is the manifestation of their desire to escape from their chronic deformities. More disturbing is the perversion of eroticism in Elena Poniatowska's story focusing on the mistress/maid relationship, in which the mistress's arrogance and sadistic contempt is coupled with her sexual need for the maid's presence. And in Teresa Ruiz Rosas's plot of the country girl betrayed by her city lover, only murder can redress injustice.

It is perhaps worth adding a few comments from the point of view of the translator. First, concerning the variety of language that reigns among Latin American authors, it is easy to think of Latin American writing as a whole, due to the common history and traditions of all its countries. In fact, setting aside Brazilian

Portuguese, the varieties of Spanish spoken and written in the remaining countries are considerable to the extent that there are words and expressions used in a given country that would not be known to readers in another country. Second, there is a richness of the style that can on some occasions appear to the English reader alarmingly poetic, when not confusing, strident, and even shocking.

Spanish is by tradition a language invested with the spirit of the baroque. The style of Latin American authors is often doubly baroque, as the Cuban writer and critic Alejo Carpentier stated several decades ago: writing within the reality of a "new world" with a tool that is not indigenous to it has made it necessary, for some at least, to pile up nouns and adjectives, seek metaphors, borrow native words, create neologisms.

One more ingredient, present in much Latin American fiction of the last fifty years, will become apparent in the texts presented here: the fascination with psychoanalysis. For no apparently clear reason, psychoanalytical theories have taken a strong hold in Latin America; witness of it is the relatively large number of Argentinean and other Latin Americans working in this field in the UK. The Argentinean author Manuel Puig, probably best known for the film *Kiss of the Spider Woman*, often allows, in the course of the novel by the same title, as much as half a page of footnotes quoting from Freud, his daughter Anna, D. J. West, Herbert Marcuse, Leon Altman, et al. This preoccupation with analyzing the psychological motivation and manifestations of people's behavior appears, sometime with ironic emphasis, in such stories as "Spick and Span" and "In Florence Ten Years Later" or, as a destructive element, in "Golden Days of a Queen of Diamonds."

Violations:
Stories of Love by
Latin American
Women

To Love or to Ingest

I am going to the local supermarket. It's on several floors and sells everything from a box of pins to a motorboat. What I like most is to arrive – there are two entrances on the ground floor – with a list in my pocket of all the things to buy for Ana's visit.

At first I had imagined that it would be inconvenient for Ana and me to live in different cities, but I soon thought otherwise, for I got pleasure from desiring her during our separation. We have no fixed dates for our meetings. In fact, thinking of it, I don't even know anything about Ana's life; all I know is that she lives in a city four hours away by plane. I had no wish to ask for her telephone number, but I gave her mine. Which she does not use. All I get from time to time is a telegram: "Meet me on Thursday at eight in the evening, Ana." That's fine by me. Any word unconnected with desire, any information that adds nothing to it and may distract us, seems unnecessary. Desire is exacting, intolerant, and despotic. It does not want to know anything unrelated to the body and its activities. Though I never told her, I appreciate the fact that she never asked any questions that had nothing to do with our desire. Why would she want to know about my work, my relatives, what my politics are, or my favorite hobby?

She asks no questions. Nor do I. I don't even know if Ana is her real name. What does it matter? What matters are the secret names we call each other, not those that appear on our identity cards.

Her telegrams arrive unexpectedly. Sometimes the doorman gives them to me, at other times they reach me by telephone. But our dates are always fixed for late in the evening. Which is good, because it gives me more time to prepare things during the day.

On the day of her arrival, I miss work. I invent some obvious excuse: I have a sore throat; my mother is not well; there is a problem with the plumbing and I have to wait for the plumber. I couldn't very well say, "I'm busy – I've got to prepare for Ana's visit." Nobody would dream of granting a day off for the most important reason in the world: a love meeting. For illness, yes; for pleasure, no.

Not that it matters. The excuse works. I get up early, have a large coffee, and, smoking a cigarette, I begin to imagine our time together. The usual, least significant items of everyday life acquire new importance. Cigarettes, for example. I choose three and place them by the bedside: after lovemaking I like to insert one – filter first – into Ana's wet vagina. The soft paper absorbs her moisture and, when I take it out, it tastes like the wet walls of her sex. I bring it to my lips and light it (sometimes it is so damp that I have trouble) and inhale deeply. No cigarette tastes so good. Its flavor, mixed with her juices, changes: it tastes slightly of seaweed.

"Women smell fishy," my boss said one day, half drunk. We were having dinner together, a working dinner, and he had had too much to drink. He said it with some repugnance, as if the smell of fish disgusted him. I pointed out that I had seen him eating large quantities of sea bass, baked salmon, and turbot. But he said that cooked fish smells different from raw. "Women smell like raw fish," he said.

Personally, I am excited by that smell. I like strong odors that can't be hidden or disguised. Seafood, for example: hard-shelled crustaceans, rosy shellfish, lustful oysters, eels sinuous like snakes. The kind of smell that remains in your hands, like a woman's. The powerful smell of cod inside her legs. I put my head between Ana's thighs and inhale deeply. A floating vapor soaks my lips, my chin, enters my nostrils, goes to my head, makes me dizzy. How can a man like a woman if he doesn't like her smell? I easily understand the ancient habit of eating the enemy: love and hatred can only

2

end with the consumption of the other. That's why pregnant women carry the fetus in their belly with blood, water, feces and their own nourishment. They love their children because they have grown inside them, sucking their secretions, feeding from their glands, fattening up on their fats and sugars.

Love is like this: a question of bodies and innards. I understand the Japanese man who killed his mistress in Paris, cut her up into small pieces, and put her in the freezer. Every day he defrosted a portion and ate it garnished with vegetables and condiments. A morsel from her arm baked with spring onions and peppers. For dessert, a breast served with a coulis of wild cherries. If women did not give birth through their vaginas – a form of defecation – they could expel their babies in their vomit. Spasmodic tremors would eject segments of apples mixed with sperm, tears, a little arm, vertebrae, a gallbladder, a hairy head, lungs. . . . The Japanese ate his woman and, by doing so, accomplished an old almost forgotten rite: ingesting what we love or hate so as to possess it completely. We also eat cows in the form of beefsteak, chicken in stews, white rabbits, and partridges.

My desire for Ana is carnal, largely physiological. Her legs, for example. I just love shaving them. I ask her not to do it herself, to come to me with all the bodily hair that God gave her. I like her to arrive complete, every part of her with its strong smell, hairs, secretions, and excretions. She stretches out on my black velvet sofa, lifts her skirt, and there are her beautiful legs, her white thighs and her bottom, covered by soft down, thicker at the top, getting finer, almost invisible, just above her knees. I run a sweet-smelling oil over her naked skin and gently rub it in. My fingers become impregnated with this unguent. Internal fluids, physiological juices, natural wax, vegetable oils. Who would want to distinguish among them? And why?

We do not communicate between our meetings. She leaves the following morning, and I don't even take her to the airport.

None of those pathetic lovers' farewells, conventional leave-takings, meaningless conversations to while the time away. None of what naïve, vulgar, or feeble people call love. But who would dare say that we do not love each other? I feel an uncontrollable passion for the cells of her body – those minute particles of cytoplasm and nucleus that form her skin. I have looked at them with a magnifying glass. Ana's epithelial tissues are arranged in small, finely edged, tessellating rhombuses. I think of her body: the innumerable cells running along her femur, the nape of her neck, her clavicles and tibias. To know where she lives, who her parents are, how much she earns, and what music she listens to when alone would not add anything to my meticulous knowledge of her skin, muscles, and glands. Apropos of music, I have included in the list of today's items James Last's *Bluebird:* pathetic and high-pitched like an Andean flute, its penetrating sound filling me with delight. I had to search through many shelves in music shops to find it. That's the way it should be: the lover chooses the elements necessary for the ritual of love with the dedication and expertise of a collector.

I shall receive her with a dish of red strawberries, which I shall burst open and let bleed over her body, some the exact size of her clitoris. It will be like a homosexual encounter, clitoris to clitoris, and the juice will flow between the swollen labia of her vagina.

On the ground floor of the supermarket, I spent some time in the toiletries department. There are smooth, slippery soaps of different colors, wrapped in cellophane. I pick three: a green one smelling of pine for the hair of her armpit, a salmon-pink one for her sex, and the lilac one – they dressed witches in lilac before they burnt them – for her back. I also buy a set of candles in the shape of water lilies, which float in a water-filled dish like a sea of amputated breasts. And Persian caviar which I will spread over her pubic hair to look like little trapped beetles. To eat her and to love her is all one thing. To touch her and to taste her. My glands mixed

4

with hers, my sweat with her sweat, my bile with her bile in the original chaos of the universe, the first magma in which you cannot separate solids from liquids, gasses from entrails, skin from bones. We are born headfirst and die in the worst of solitudes: that of a broken-down body which no longer finds echo in another body. I wonder if that's why people die, because they can no longer find echoes in another body.

My boss said yesterday at lunch that he is happy in his marriage and that his wife understands him. I stifled my laughter. What is there to understand in this fat, greasy man who swallows enormous quantities of processed foods – margarine, lowfat yogurts, dry carrots – and who goes three times a week to a gym and once a year follows a course of meditation in a fashionable spa. I do not trust fat people; they turn their repressed desires into fat. They sweat in the sauna, not in bed. I, on the other hand, am not fat. I would consider it an offence to the woman who loves me. Ana's hands running up and down my back have no problem in finding the lines of my bones under a layer of skin. She touches them with pleasure, caresses them, counts them.

"I would love to make a meal of your 'spare ribs,'" she tells me.

She licks my nipples and sticks her tongue in my navel just like animals lick each other to heal their wounds or show their love. While I'm waiting for her, I jump around the living room like a chimpanzee, beat my chest, roar, go around on all fours. The animal inside gets ready for the feast. The other day I read in an American magazine that this is a kind of therapy. I laughed. The Yankee therapist who recommended such treatment thought that he was discovering the prophylactic value of reverting, for a few minutes each day, to the animal we once were. Forget this and death will follow. Our weakened entrails will burst open and speak up, at our cost, for the time they have remained silent.

I do not want Ana's death. As long as we love each other with our primitive bodies, with the oil that protects our skin from the cold, the hair in our noses that keeps out the bacteria, the beating liver that filters the toxic substances, I know that she will not die. Only those bodies that have remained silent for a long time die.

But one day she will get married. In her unnamed city, four hours away by plane, she will contract marriage like one contracts an illness, a social illness. And her body folded over, her ovaries on heat, her swelling glands, they will gather together to multiply – she will grow with child. A curious form of parthenogenesis from which a second Ana or Ano will emerge, to comply with the species' destiny. As a man I cannot split or multiply myself, be the host of another being. As a male I can only aspire to eating, annulling another body. Reproduction is not my lot. I can only die or kill: I cannot be two in one by any process other than death.

From the dictionary: *Ana* – Prefix to indicate of each an equal quantity.

So your name is a mistake: we shall never be an equal quantity. Yet with our differences we shall love each other till destruction. Which of us will survive? You, to give birth. Women lose interest in men once they become pregnant. The stranger we have inserted into their bodies will eventually lead to our exile, our exclusion. We all become the orphans of pregnant women. That's why we turn to other women, the childless, the empty ones who need to be filled. No doubt, when you no longer come, I shall become depressed. Depression is not, as some think, a sickness of the mind; it is a sickness of a body that has lost desire, the ability to desire, deprived for some reason of the object of its desire. In this state of no desire, it slowly begins to decay. My hair will no longer shine with the gloss of desire; my back will bend with age; my skin will acquire that whitish hue of the dead, which some civilizations have wrongly thought superior; my hands will cease to feel and my nose to smell primeval substances in the crevices of another body. I will age, because when you suckle your child, he will deprive me of my nourishment.

Still, the time of this future confrontation has not yet come. I pick up the telephone and dial my office. Ask for my boss. He does not answer straight away. He is a very busy man with thousands of details to attend to, in between ingesting his various pills (an anabolic steroid for digestion, a sugar-coated one for the circulation, and vitamins to offset stress).

"It's Carlos," I say. "I have a headache and feel dizzy."

"It must have been something you ate that didn't suit you," he says, happy to advise me. "Take an Alka-Seltzer and rest. And above all, no solid food for the rest of the day."

Solid food, I think. Ana's buttocks flambées à l'orange.

"I won't," I say hanging up the phone.

Or perhaps a light dish of cerveaux en vinaigrette.

Translated from the Spanish by Psiche Hughes

English Love

M came on Sunday – no, not Sunday, Saturday. There I was, Nora García, eating with my mother, when the black dog – a chow chow – howls and warns us that something is there, under the door. The maid picks it up and hands it to me; it's probably one of those advertisements trying to sex up the sale of a fridge, Christmas fare, or the installation of an intercom, I tell myself. But I am wrong. It is a letter (a love letter?), unsealed, on ordinary paper; the characters are precise, formal. Impeccable. Legible English writing, the result of patient work and of the rulers that public-school teachers or matrons used to punish little boys whose letters lacked elegance, neatness, and precision. (If only I had had such a teacher! It's enough to look at my writing to understand why.) The note starts with the usual formula: Dear Nora.

I don't take much notice. I see that it's a strange declaration of love – of a rather literary kind – that, to make matters worse, or better (according to how one looks at it), alludes to a book by Graham Greene, *Travels with My Aunt*, as if I knew it. It seems that such an aunt was very much like me. Had nobody told me? No, of course, any resemblance with any aunt is purely coincidental. Given the situation, I go on eating and paying attention to the frustrated idyll of my dogs. She is still small, very excitable, a lion cub, affectionate and greedy; he is black, bony, with tousled fur. She's in heat, he's in love. Unfortunately, they're separated, like Tristan and Isolde. They look at each other through the window-pane, yelp, scratch, whine, breaking my heart. I look at my letter with nostalgia, nothing romantic in it, nothing like the medieval passion that my dogs are living now, flesh and blood. My little

9

letter is in a very good English hand, and is from an Englishman who, on top of it all, is a spy, like Graham Greene, a traveler like Graham Greene, Catholic and cult, like Graham Greene, aloof and public-school educated, like Graham Greene. Eton? Cambridge? He speaks with tight lips (though he has been living in Mexico for over twenty years), his *r*s are vocalized, aspirated; he hardly moves his mouth when he pronounces words of love. Are they words of love? How does he write them? Holding the pen close to the paper, just as he holds his lips when he pronounces his *r*s? I study the note with calm. It announces that he loves me; actually, the word is never mentioned – has the paper eaten it up, just as he eats up his *r*s? It suggests that we should travel together, that he will lead me through the most intricate mazes of my own city, places I definitely don't know. I am sure I don't, but I confess I am alarmed by these journeys, the business of the aunt and the perfect English handwriting.

I let a few days go by and, when I decide to speak to him, he's not there. I leave a message. Hello M, this is Nora, Nora García. In the afternoon he calls me in faultless Spanish. He will come that evening but not alone, sorry, he will come with an English woman, a famous writer, if I don't mind. Of course I don't, I say, do come. My dogs are still kept apart and sad. She in heat, youthfully so, intact and virgin; he's three years older, also a virgin. Talking to M, I look at them out of the corner of my eyes. I'm sad, I can't understand it. Why can't he come alone? Why are the dogs also sad? That very night I am going to a party at the house of a Mexican, friend of an English woman, friend of mine, here on a visit. (She adores us, our sun, the way it arouses people – whom? builders? pedestrians? young snobs?)

I get ready, avoiding a too loud color scheme, being too Mexican, overdressed. I switch on discreet lighting and wait. The frustrated idyll keeps me entertained. She's in the house now, and he's in the garden. The yelping continues, like my waiting: ten past seven, yelp; twenty-five past, yelp; forty-three past, yelp; fifty past, the bell. He's very apologetic. Hello, Nora, he says, and kisses me; his lips just touch mine, or rather the left side of my mouth. A fat English woman enters with him, hair all over the place, pink cheeks, breasts down to her ankles. *Travels without Maps*, by Graham Greene. Black naked English women in a garden? She wears a flowery skirt of indefinite colors, a celestial blouse, ideal attire for a rainy day in England or for trimming the roses in the garden on a wet Mexican day without roses. They are not alone; another English woman accompanies them on a quick visit to Mexico before returning to Ecuador? Peru? Bolivia? where her husband is posted. The second woman is wearing relics of the Victorian age; her hair short, sprayed down, a blue cashmere sweater, white blouse, a short pearl necklace around her short neck, tartan skirt – green, white, and dark blue. Moccasins with low heels. She has just come back from England where she has left her children in several public schools according to their ages. As in *The Towers of Mallory*? I ask her. Yes, they are going to have a lot of fun. They produce many children and send them all to boarding schools to learn to write little letters in impeccable handwriting, like the one M sent me.

He is sitting in front of me with his two typically English ladies. Differently attired but equally trapped in the implacable pyramid of language and public-school accent – just as an English writer will tell me, weeks later, as I am sitting by his side next to his formidable wife and some Mexicans who pronounce English with the shameless accent of Americans eating Kansas City steak. M takes a whisky on the rocks, the lady writer is on her second whisky with a dash of cold water, and the other is drinking a sherry, medium dry. We talk of children – the Victorian lady's, and mine who can't stand boarding schools English style. As we carry on in that low continuum, that imperceptible muttering that emerges between closed teeth and stiff upper lip (male and female), my English deteriorates rapidly: more and more it becomes

11

a pitiful whisper lost amid the endless yelping of the dogs. I get up, leaving the conversation behind me, open the door and let the dog in, quickly ushering the little bitch out. Filled with melancholia I feed on her frustrated love and accompany it to the rhythm of mine, more frustrated by the minute, if less lamented. What breed are they? I am asked. Chows, I say. (Can't you see they are not English?)

They ask for more sherry, more whisky on the rocks, and more whisky with cold water (though I only have ice and lukewarm water). The lady writer is now talking of animals, not dogs but chickens and roosters and their sexuality. Her accent is so perfect, so tight, like M's or Laurence Olivier's. I can't hear them any more; I misunderstand them as I listen to the language of my dogs. I catch a phrase here and there: philosophy has classified, enumerated, different methods to discover the sex (the gender) of chickens and roosters. All you have to do is to put a hand between their legs and establish what is hanging there among the feathers. And she says so in such a serious and elegant fashion in her impeccable accent. Suddenly, almost without our noticing, she changes the topic of conversation. The dogs are still looking at each other through the window; they scratch and yelp, and the male begins to rub against my knees, laddering my stockings. The woman with droopy breasts is now wishing to establish, with precise, Aristotelian logic, if the sculpture on the mantelpiece of the apostle James is wood or ceramic. Wood, I say, decorated wood from the eighteenth century; an old piece I found in Antigua, Guatemala, I explain, as I drink my second sherry. Without rhyme or reason, we are now involved in a profound discussion on wood, its quality, veins, color, and properties. Cherry wood is red, I say. No, she contests. Then cedar is red. Wrong again, she assures me. She was in New England (this is her first visit to Mexico, in fact, the first time she has come to Latin America, though she has been to North America many times) and once had a drink (whisky water?) on a "marvelous" terrace. She says so, just like Father Bartolomé de las Casas who, faced with something beautiful, extraordinary, and lacking the vocabulary to describe it, used the term "marvelous." So does this lady philosopher, or writer, with droopy breasts, as she talks with me and M and the other English woman, the post-Victorian, while my dogs in love yelp and her children grow accustomed to their imprisonment. That terrace or veranda, she continues, was made of wood, "marvelous" wood, unpainted, unvarnished, just polished. And it was gray, she adds triumphantly, gray like the light of the moon shining on an object, giving it a silvery glow. That's exactly what that "marvelous" wood was like. Cedar, her jubilant voice stresses, is not red, it is gray like steel, like silver.

Long silence. M is saying nothing. The dogs appear to have resigned themselves to their fate, the tragic destiny of solitary lovers; the mother of the children installed in several public schools sips her third sherry. I help myself to another, and serve another whisky – weak – to the English woman who loves wood and classifies it, just as, no doubt, she classifies languages and human races. Hearing her talk about wood that does not deteriorate I lift my eyes and look at my rotting, chewed-up beams, and I am filled with "marvel." I slavishly begin to copy the English woman and, in my turn, I too imitate Father de las Casas and Columbus, and experience their sense of the "marvelous" in the face of the American Paradise and the heavenly innocence of the Indians, while I listen to the termites destroying the perfectly ordinary wood of my house, which looks old but isn't. Once again the conversation languishes; I am lost between the colors of wood and the threat of its destruction. The conversation has deteriorated, interrupted suddenly by a pitiful howl. It's the little bitch once again inside the house; the dog is in the garden. M stammers, drops his *r*s or rather swallows them, just as I would like to swallow the termites before they devour all the beams in my house. Stunned by this thought,

13

the howling, the third sweet sherry, the soft muttering, and the sense of decay, I have completely lost the thread.

M gets up, apologizes again most unnecessarily for arriving late: he's like any other Mexican now, or rather like one of the railway employees at Paddington, Liverpool Street, or Victoria Station, announcing over the speakers that the train due to arrive at five on the dot is not arriving on the dot at all. At the very moment when he reaches the door, surrounded by his formidable English women, I take the opportunity to invite them to the party given by that friend of another English woman, friend of mine, a largish, pleasant, easygoing blonde with working-class legs, perfect public-school accent, and great sense of (English) humor. No, they say, it's not proper to gatecrash, like this, somebody else's party, without a formal invitation. They will go out to supper. Would I go with them? No, no, no, thank you, it's late, and I couldn't bear any more conversation on wood, rain, the sex of birds; thank you, no. I take them to the door. The writer stops. Facing her by the door, the sculpture of Saint James, my guardian. She looks at it attentively, touches it, and asks: What kind of wood? Ordinary pine, I say; deteriorates rapidly. A chap who carves holy images made it. He is a barman now at a hotel in town. The dogs' idyll continues as ever; mine finishes now, amid the colors and the deterioration of wood.

The following day I call M. He left me so frustrated. I stroke the paper (plain, unbleached). No answer. No answer the next day either. For many days I repeat the same process with no better results. He left me confused, incapable of resolving the simple elementary mysteries of the color of wood and the face of English love. I'm a poor, obtuse imitation of Dr. Watson.

The following week I have dinner with another famous British writer, many prizes, including the Nobel. We talk, drink, the conversation moves on to literature; somebody asks him if he knew T. S. Eliot? More or less, he says, a pause and then, we shared the same publishers and, once, when we turned up at the same cocktail party, he talked for an hour about umbrellas.

My two dogs are together now; they give each other little nips. They sniff, lick; they are happy. I have the little letter among my perfumed handkerchiefs, the letter that begins, in a perfect English hand: Dear Nora.

I haven't heard from M again.

Translated from the Spanish by Psiche Hughes

The Fall

"Holy Mother, it's still raining – bloody, Holy Mary. Why does it rain so much?" Words too harsh for the soft voice, for the sweet saliva, that taste of humble black sounds. That's why he's only thinking them: he could never say them aloud. Though just the thought is bad enough, too ugly for the white conscience of a black man. He has always thought and spoken differently, more like a lover.

"Help me, Holy Virgin, White Rose on the bush. Help a poor nigger who has killed that brute of a white man, who has just done this bad thing. My Only Rose, Heart of Sweet Almonds, help this negro, give him a chance, Limpid Rose in the Garden."

But he has no luck tonight. The icy rain continues and he is soaked to the bones, deep down where the cold hurts. He lost one of his shoes in the mud, and his toes poke out from the other one. Wherever there is a sharp stone, his toes hit against it, never against a rounded one. But hitting the stone is nothing, what really hurts is the whipping pain that shoots up the limbs of his body and returns once again to the toes and goes on hurting, without pause. It's then that the black man cannot understand how his white rose can do this to him. His sweetheart should have warned him about the sharp stone. And should not have allowed so much rain and cold tonight.

The black man's hands are deep in his pockets, his hat down over his ears, the old suit held together as far as the few remaining buttons permit. Not a suit, really, a wet rag slippery and shining like spittle, the weave modeling and revealing the harmonious curves of his black body. As he bends under the weight of the rain, the lines of his shoulders become more pronounced: a sculpture that color alone could never have defined.

And besides, he goes on thinking, She should have made nightfall earlier. He had asked for it all day, with not a corner for a nigger to hide his fear. And finally the lovely White Rose had sent the dark.

The man's step is as slow and steady as the rain, doesn't speed up or ease off. It's as if they – he and the rain – knew each other too well to disagree. One against the other, but with no violence, the patter of rain beating in time with the step of an ill-fated negro.

There it is, finally, the place where lies his last feverish hope. The brilliant lanterns of his wide eyes would not have beamed so bright fifty yards from paradise. The half-demolished house is there in the dark. He has never gone inside it. He only knows of it from hearsay. More than once he had been told about this shelter, but nothing more.

"Immaculate Virgin!"

This time he has called to his rose out loud. Violent lightning has just revealed his tall bony frame and his blackness in the black of the night. Next comes the blast from the sky, a dry cracking sound as painful as hitting his toe once again. He touches his thighs through the holes in his pockets. He's still here on this earth. He feels the simple, quiet joy of a black man still alive. And of course he has seen the house more clearly. He could swear that he's seen it shaking to its foundations in the blast. But the ramshackle old building has gotten back on its feet like a woman after a dizzy spell. All around it is in ruin. The brothels standing along the river had been swept clean. Only the rubble remains of the dives that nestled there in the past. Yet that fragment still stands, by some inexplicable whim. He looks at it appreciatively, a handsome ruin all lost in its solitude, in its closed mysterious silence. And now not only can he see it, he can even touch it, if he wants to.

18

But as often happens when we reach what we have so much de-
sired, he doesn't dare. He has walked and suffered so much to get
to it, that now that it stands in front of him it doesn't seem real, he
can't violate it. Yet it is only the ruin of a house: the remains of
walls on two sides, desolate heaps of trash and mud. It reappears
with each flash of lightning, showing vertical cracks, a low door, a
window in the front and another on the side.

The black man, frightened, knocks at the door, as if it were a
sacrilege; his fingers, hardened like stone by the cold, ache. It is
still raining. He knocks again but nobody comes. He needs cover,
but the outside of the house, without an overhang, offers none.
No welcoming refuge. Walking in the rain was different; confront-
ing the downpour from the falling sky is something else, not the
real rain. The real rain is what trees, stones, and all motionless
bodies learn to bear. That's when you can say that it is raining inside your very self, that the whole world of water is weighing down
on you, destroying, dissolving your existence. He knocks for the
third time, with hard frozen fingers, a black man's onyx fingers,
tender and rosy at the tips. And again he beats for a fourth time
with an angry fist. Yet the black man is mistaken, he thinks that the
door opens in response to his louder knock. In fact, four knocks
are part of the household code, and then a man appears with a
smoky lamp.

"Master, please, let a poor nigger come in."

"Come in, then, you wretch."

And he closes the door behind him and lifts the glass of the
sooty lamp as high as he can. The black man is as tall as if on stilts,
while the owner is unfortunately very short. The black man sees
his face, white with long vertical lines like chalk etched by nails.
A brutish scar of unmistakable origin runs up from the corner of
his lips to his left eyebrow, following the curve of his thin lips. It
makes the mouth look huge as if turning upward to the eyebrows.
Narrow, sharp eyes with no lashes and a squashed nose.

After observing him at length the new arrival says, "How much is it, Master?" his voice like molasses.

"You can choose: ten for the camp bed, two on the floor. Hurry up and decide, you stupid nigger," says the white man roughly, as he shields the lamp with his hand.

That was the tariff: ten cents or two, but the luxury accommodation, the single camp bed, almost always remained unoccupied.

The black man looks at the floor, no vacancies; a bestial gathering, its collective snoring rising, solid, its many variations like night tunes from a swamp.

"I'll take the floor, master," he says humbly, bowing his head. The scarred man lifts his lamp and snakes his way among the bodies. Taking the same turns, the black man follows him like a dog. As yet the owner is not interested in knowing whether the new arrival has the money. He will find out once the other falls asleep, though similar searches normally prove fruitless. People with money only come here by mistake. This is a house for beggars, the last refuge for the night when no other door opens. He can hardly remember an occasion when he rented out the famous bed, at such high price; it has now become his own special accommodation.

"Here you are, that's where you lie," he says as he stops, his voice piercing and cold like the slash on his face. "You can undress, or not, as it suits you. Your place is here between these two piles. You are lucky, but if somebody else turns up you will have to make him space by your side. This section is a bed for two, three, or twenty men."

From his height of six feet three the black man looks down: among the rubbish on that stretch of floor there remains for some unknown reason a kind of hollow, soft and warm, as if between two outstretched bodies.

He is about to undress, to become one more body amid that heaving crowd of backs, bellies, and snoring, of smells and brutish dreams, of whistling and laments. But just then, as the owner is blowing out the light by his camp bed, the black man discovers the image of the White Rose, a small oil flame flickering by it on a shelf in the wall. Right in front of him.

"Master, please!"

"Be quiet, will you?"

"Tell me," continues the other, not at all put out, "do you believe in the Immaculate Child?"

The scarred man answers from his camp bed with a cold laugh that cuts the air. "You are such an ignorant nigger! What do you mean, 'Do I believe?' I keep the statue just in case it works, in case it has some power and can stop this ruin from falling apart."

And once again he begins to laugh with that sound that is like the scar on his face. But he has to stop: a tremor, which seems to be coming from the bottom of the earth, shakes the house. What thunder, the black man thinks; it feels different inside the building as if it had boomed inside his belly, his very life. The wind and rain are now twice as strong. The window on the side of the house is the worst hit; it shakes as if prey to an uncontrollable seizure.

But now, above all, the smell of the black man rises. It seems to be swallowing all the other sounds and smells, having beaten them all in open battle.

How to sleep? With his clothes on? Like sleeping in water. With his clothes off, skin and bone as he is, soaked in icy rain? He decides in favor of the wet naked skin, which is beginning to warm up. So he stretches down in that hollow, naked as the day he was born. The light from the little lamp in front of the Virgin is becoming warmer and brighter, fed by the oil in the dark, the same oil of the black man's skin. Stretching at an angle from the wall of the Virgin to the next hangs a kind of dirty gauze, a ghostly floating object that undulates with each gust of wind. A remnant that has grown in the house. Each time the wind grows outside the rag shakes, gathering vertiginous speed into a dizzy dance. With his ears closed, the black man thinks, Even if I were deaf, I wouldn't liberate myself from the wind. I would see it in that shaking web, Sweet Mother of God, I would die seeing it.

He begins to shiver. His forehead is on fire, and so, from time to time, is the whole of his body. Then it's freezing again, and shivering, and sweating. He tries to cover himself. But with what? There is no remedy. He will have to bear it all in his nakedness, unprotected, stretched out in that hollow. How long will he go on in this terrible state, shivering, sweating, unprotected against the cold? He can't tell. And on top of it, that ache that is knifing his back. Must shut his eyes and try to sleep. Sleeping, he might forget it all. There is a lot to forget, besides his miserable body. Above all, what he has done this very day with his own hands, those hands that add more pain to his body.

But first he wants to look at the Little Virgin. There she is, sweet and tender, all in white, watching over their sleep. The black man thinks darkly, How can she stay among such a lost crowd, this dirty human mass, breathing in that awful smell of impurity, crimes, vices, and ugly dreams rising from the bodies in rags? Frightened, he looks at that overwhelming blend of humanity, lice, and sins, stretched snoring there on the ground below her gentle light.

And what about him? Thinking about himself he remembers that he has no clothes on; he is the worst of all. They at least are not showing the Little Virgin, as he is, their flesh, their naked shame. He must hide it then, cover himself somehow, not to offend the eyes of the Immaculate Mary. He tries to, but he can't move. Cold, fever, shivers, and the ache in his back; his will is dead. Can only sleep. But he is not able to. Perhaps he never will be. He will remain forever in this hollow, without crying out that he is dying, without being able to pray to the Good Virgin, ask her to forgive his jet-colored nakedness, his skin and bones, his invincible smell, and, worst of all, what his hands have done today.

At this moment, what he never imagined possible happens. The White Rose slowly begins to come down from the shelf. High up there she seemed small, like a doll, hard and plain; but now, as she descends, she grows in size, her flesh shapes up, softens, and becomes alive. The negro is about to die of fear and astonishment. It's all too much, beyond him. He tries to pinch himself to be sure that he is really there, to have something to hang onto, but he can't. Apart from the pain and the cold, he has no other sense of his reality; the rest is incredible, remote, as in a world and a time that are not his own and are lost to him. All except this woman coming down.

The White Rose will not stop. There is in her walk and her look a fatal determination, as in the flowing of water or the course of light reaching the world. But what terrifies him most is the direction of her steps: is she coming toward him, just to him, the most naked and dirty of all? Yet there she is by his side. He can see her little shoes of gilded clay and the border of her celestial veil.

The black man wants to sit up. In vain. Fear, shivering, and shame are nailing him down, his back on the ground. At this moment he hears her voice, the sweetest honey he ever tasted in his life.

"Tristan!"

Yes, this was his name, a long time ago, a time left behind the door – what is real is that the Virgin Mary has come down, and those are her feet of clay, and that is the border of her veil. He must answer, or he will die. Must speak, show that he recognizes her presence of flowers. He tries to swallow: just a drop of thick, bitter saliva, but enough.

"Is it you, White Rose on the Bush?"

"Yes, Tristan. Can't you move?"

"No, Blessed Child, I don't know what is happening. It all remains up here in my thinking of it and doesn't seem to come down to my doing. But I can't believe it is really you, Limpid Pearl, I just can't."

"Yes it is me, Tristan, you have to believe it."

At this moment the incredible happens. The Virgin kneels by the side of the man. It has always been the other way. Now it is the Virgin who bows down in front of him.

"Holy Mother of God, don't do this, Single Rose Flowering on the Bush, please don't do it!"

"Yes, Tristan, I will not just kneel, which is quite painful; tonight I will do what I never dared doing, and you will have to help me."

"Me, helping you, Lily of the Water? With these hands that can't do anything, except that today. . . . Oh, I can't tell you, Little Lady, what they have done today. Forgive me, Pure Lily. Forgive this good black man, who has become a bad black man on such a black day.

"Tristan, give me your hand with which you have killed."

"How do you know he was killed by a negro?"

"Don't speak like a heretic, Tristan, give me that hand."

"I can't lift it."

"Then I shall come to your hand," she answers, and her voice sounds more and more like a living person's.

And now another scandal occurs in the coming of the Virgin: she brings her waxy lips to the hard bony hand of the negro and kisses it. No woman has ever kissed it like this.

"Holy Mother of God, I can't take this."

"Yes, Tristan, I have kissed that hand with which you have killed. And do you know why? Because it was my voice you heard inside you saying, Be strong, squeeze him tighter, finish him off, don't hesitate."

"You, Mother of Baby Jesus?"

"Yes, Tristan, you have just said it. Because they killed my son and would kill him again if he came back. And I can't take the hypocrisy any more. I've had enough of pearls and prayers, of tears, incense, and hymns. One had to be the first to pay for it, and you helped me. I have been very patient, and finally I know the time has come. My child, my poor sweet child, sacrificed in vain. How I cried, soaking his lacerated body in my tears. But you, Tristan, you don't know the worst of it."

"Tell me, Sweet Mother."

"I can't cry for his loss anymore. They have made me of marble and wax, they have carved me in wood, gold, ivory, and lies, and I can no longer cry. I have to go on living their lies, with this stupid smile they have put on my face. I was not like they painted me, Tristan, less beautiful, perhaps, but different. Let me tell you why I have come down."

"Do so, tell everything to this poor nigger."

"My plan is going to scare you, Tristan."

"I am dead scared already, Candid Lily, yet I am no dead nigger, I am still alive."

"Well, then, Tristan," the Virgin explains, her voice becoming firmer by the minute, more and more human, "I am going to lie by your side. After all, the owner of this place did say that there was room for two in this hollow."

"Don't, please, Mother of Jesus, my tongue is becoming paralyzed, and I won't be able to beg you again."

"Do you know what is happening to you, Tristan? You have been praying since you saw me. Nobody has ever prayed such poetry to me before."

"I will invent for you the sweetest tune, will steal from the singing reeds all their words and their tears, but please don't lie by the side of this bad nigger."

"Oh, yes I will. Just watch me!"

And the black man watches that doll-like image stretch alongside him, silk and beads rustling, the perfume of time and virginity in her hair.

"Now comes the most important task for you, Tristan. You

must take my clothing off. Start with my shoes, they are an instrument of torture; so rigid they murder my feet. It doesn't worry them that I have been standing throughout the centuries. Take them off, please, Tristan, I can't stand them anymore."

"Oh, yes, I will free your aching feet with my sinful hands. This I will do with pleasure, Pure Lady."

"What a relief, Tristan. But not enough. Look at my ridiculous feet made out of wax. Just feel the wax."

"Yes, Little Lady of the Waxen Feet, they are made of wax."

"But I am going to tell you what really matters. Inside the wax, Tristan, my feet are made of flesh."

"Oh, Holy Mother, I am dying!"

"And I am flesh all over underneath this wax."

"Stop, stop, Dear Mother, go back on the shelf. This nigger can't bear that the Holy Mother, made flesh, lies with him in this hollow. Go back, Sweet Rose, back to the place of the Candid Rose."

"Sorry, Tristan, I will not go back. Once a Virgin has come down from her pedestal she can't go back. You must melt all the wax. I don't want to go on being the most Immaculate of all. I want to be the real mother of the child they murdered. I must be able to walk, hate, and cry on the earth. And for this I be must be made of flesh, not of cold, dead wax."

"And how can I melt your wax, Sweet Lily?"

"Touch me, Tristan, caress me. Until now your hands were paralyzed, but now that I have kissed them you can use them. You can see the importance of a caress. Go ahead, touch my waxen feet, and you will see how their shape softens."

"Yes, my Sweet Solitary Pearl, I agree, feet must be free. A nigger knows this. Free and of real flesh. Even if hard stones do hurt them. There, I am caressing them, and already I feel what's happening, Holy Virgin, I feel it, see, Blessed Mother, see how my fingers are now dripping with wax."

"And now touch my feet, really touch them Tristan."

"Two live gardenias, your feet are like gardenias."

"That's not enough. Carry on, free my legs."

"What, the legs of the Perfect Rose? I can't bear it. I can't go on melting your wax. It frightens me. It frightens a nigger too much."

"Carry on, Tristan, carry on."

"Only up to the knees, Imprisoned Lady. No higher. It is as far as this negro can go, committing such a terrible offence. I swear I will stop there. Cut my hands off, Mother of the Golden Baby, and make a negro forget that he ever had these hands and with them touched the stem of the Holy Flower. Sharpen the knife in blood and cut them off."

A violent clap of thunder shakes the night. The windows crash and bang, and once more the house rocks like a boat.

"Do you hear? See what is happening tonight. If you don't keep melting my wax, there will be no other chance for me. Keep going, hurry, reach up to the thigh. I need the entire leg."

"Sweet thighs of my black perdition, here they come, warm and soft like lizards in the winter sun. But I can't bear it any more, Little Virgin. See, I am crying. These tears are made of the aching blood of a negro."

"Do you hear, Tristan, do you see? The house is shaking again. Why are you afraid of a thigh? Keep melting my wax."

"But I am getting close to the Golden Narcissus, Little Lady. This is the locked garden. I can't, I won't."

"Touch it Tristan, touch that too, especially that. When the wax melts there, you won't need to go any further. The wax over my breast, my back, my tummy will melt on its own. Do it, Tristan. I need it all."

"No, Little Lady. It is the Golden Narcissus. I can't."

"It will go on being the Golden Narcissus. You don't think that if you touch it, it will cease to be so?"

"But it is not just touching, it's that one can want it all, with all the madness of a negro's blood. Have pity, Little Lady. This

27

negro does not want to lose himself and begs you with tears to let him go."

"Do it. Look me in the eyes and do it."

It is then that the negro lifts his eyes toward those of the Virgin and meets those bright forget-me-nots sparkling with celestial fire like the burning of the chimera. And he can't but obey. Let her consume him with the flames of her power and his torture.

"I knew it. Why did I do it? Why did I touch it? Now I want to go inside. I need to bury myself in the moisture of the garden. The poor negro can't take it any more. Look, you Imprisoned Lady, how the life of this nigger shakes, how his mad blood rises to drown him. I knew I shouldn't have touched it. Let me enter that tight circle, Forbidden Lady, and then kill this negro in the midst of his downfall."

"No, Tristan, you can't. You have done something much greater, don't you know?"

"Yes Sweet Palm of my black dreams. I know what a horrible thing I have done."

"You don't know it really. You have freed a virgin; what you want now is of no importance. What matters is for a man to know how to free a virgin. This is the true glory of a man, whether he is able or not to enter her."

"But this is too hard for the poor head of a nigger. It may not be for the clear head of someone down from Heaven. . . ."

"Tristan, what you don't know is that you are about to die."

"To die? What does that mean?"

"Have you forgotten about death, Tristan? Only for this would I give you the Golden Narcissus of your desire. A man deserves to enter the garden when, by the side of a woman, he forgets about death. But I will not give it to you. Forget it."

"And then, Pure Moon in the sky, will you give it to somebody else once you go walking in the world on your feet of flesh below the stems of sweet hyacinth?"

"What do you mean? Are you mad? Do you think the mother of the child they murdered would go about rewarding them? My only reality lies in this: they have taken my son from me, but I remain intact. They cannot spoil me. They will never learn what it is to suffer with desire. Tell me, Tristan, do you suffer more from being a negro or for being a man?"

"Oh, Little Star above the Island, let me think it out clearly in the darkness of a nigger's mind."

The man sinks his head between the woman's breast, now turned to flesh, to clear his thoughts. He breathes in the perfume of flowers in heat, snuggles in their maternal softness; then, in a state of madness, he screams.

"I had forgotten, Dear Mother. It came back to me there among the flow of your childless milk. They are going to lynch me. I have touched one of their people. Let me die, sweet Little Lady, let me escape. It is not for being a man that I suffer. Let me slip away, release me."

"Don't scream like this, Tristan. You will wake all the men asleep on the floor," she answers, her voice rocking him gently like a lullaby. "Fear not. Nothing will happen to you. Do you hear how the wind blows? The house has not fallen yet because I was there. But something worse can happen, even in my presence."

"What is that?"

"I'll tell you: they have looked for you everywhere. This is the only place left. They have saved it for last, as usual. In a few minutes they will arrive, they will come because you killed that brute of a man. That you are agonizing naked in this hovel will be of no avail. They will walk on top of the other men and will throw themselves upon you and drag you out by an arm or a leg."

"Oh, Mother of Mine. Don't allow it."

"No, I will not allow it. How could I? You are the man who helped me come free of that imprisoning wax. I can't forget such a man."

"And how will you stop them from capturing me?"

"All I need is to walk out of that window, now I have feet, now you have given them to me," she answers in his ear. "They will knock. You know the code. At the fourth knock the man gets up from his camp bed. They come for you. I have already fled. If you were not destined to die, I would take you with me and together we would jump out of the window. But in this, the Father has more power than I. You cannot escape your death. All I can do for you is to stop them from catching you alive."

"And then, Dear Mother?" asks the negro kneeling down in spite of his weakness.

"You know, Tristan, what will happen to this house once I am away?"

"Listen. They are knocking for the first time."

"At the second knock, Tristan, we embrace each other," whispers the woman, falling on her knees.

Hearing the knocks, the man on the camp bed has gotten to his feet. He lights the lamp.

"Now, Tristan."

The negro embraces the virgin. Breathes in her real hair, smelling of woman's hair, holds her woman's cheek tight against his face.

Third knock at the door. The scarred man weaves his way amid the sleeping men on the floor. These are not normal knocks, he knows that. These are knocks with a full stomach and a gun in hand. At this moment the woman opens the window on the side of the house. Slim and bright like a half moon, she only needs a small gap to fly out. A sad, feeble breath of wind takes her into the night.

"Mother, Mother, do not leave me! I have heard the fourth knock, and now I know what death means. Any death, but not their death."

"Be quiet, stupid nigger," says the other man in a muffled voice.

"I bet it's you they're coming for. Son of a bitch, I knew you were no good."

At this moment it all happens. Like stones with eyes they come in. Holding their lamps they go straight for the negro, kicking and stepping over the remaining men as if they were rotten fruit. A wind from hell comes in with them. The ruined house begins to shake, as it had done already various times during the night. But the virgin is no longer there. The sound of a skeleton cracking into pieces, of a world coming apart – the sound that precedes a total demolition.

Suddenly it crashes down on top of them all, those dead with sleep on the floor, and those who have come to take them away.

The rain has stopped, of course, and the bare wind blows more freely now, harder. It licks up the dust with its tongue. The dust of destruction.

Translated from the Spanish by Psiche Hughes

The Sea from the Window

There are thirteen people in the hospital ward. All display inconceivable blemishes and monstrous deformations; slaves all to rare illnesses, condemned to a life of suffering. They have been living here for some time, most likely will never leave.

There are no letters, presents, or visits for them; that's the way it is. Still, the outside world does not entirely forget them. From time to time they think of these victims of vile crimes and terrible injustices living in a state of fear and feverish insomnia. Atoning for their guilt. Having abandoned the human condition and accepting without struggle their part in the arrogant lineage of monsters, they are trapped, as if in a magic circle.

Yet to be a creature of fantasy, of almost mythic origin and to be, by some devious order, chained to a bed, or a tripod, or an IV bag, while daily receiving the respect and understanding of one's equals, is not so intolerable. It is easier to accept than being a lunatic or leper or beggar, or object of normal people's sickening pity and unconcealed fear. Better than being a starving petty thief at the mercy of justice. Or depending on the doubtful goodness of religious fanatics and virtuous women, or incompetent governments bent on protecting outcasts of the human herd.

They are really isolated, these thirteen. Safe in a warm world of their own where, though tormented by their suffering, they still experience the strength of sure love, transparent and unchanging, bound by generous friendship tighter than knots, without shameful envy, fear, or tearful jealousy.

All the men are a little smitten by Ada the Needle. She has no hair, and her translucent skin clings tightly to her bones; but her face remains miraculously intact and rosy despite the constant slow mutilations suffered in a former life at the hands of some skilled torturer in a prison basement. She has lost her speech, but she can still hear that Jerico loves her more than anyone, composing songs for her to stem the silent flow of her bitter tears: ballads of the glittering moonlit sea, children's rhymes, and swelling verses soft as moss.

Chief Balloon is so extraordinarily fat his huge bed must be mounted on a metal base on wheels. It takes three singularly strong male nurses, immune to fear and compassion, to move him. He is the oracle, the know-all in matters of gastronomy, expert narrator of imaginary banquets and feasts. He knows by heart hundreds of recipes and, with a deliberate and unctuous voice, devoutly describes the seasoning of the world's most fabulous dishes to the great pleasure of those who listen and dream with him. With emphatic gestures he pretends to stuff pheasants, mix exquisite sauces with sour cream, tarragon, the zest of lemon, and white wine. He prepares aromatic jasmine tea, goes into raptures at the perfumed consistency of pepper and coriander, the perfect transparency of syrup, and the airy froth of his favorite punch. Chief Balloon's stomach, stretched out of all proportion, can only tolerate unseasoned baby food, warm milk, and rye bread.

There is Gaston the Night, sherry-colored eyes dazzling under his hood, magnificent teeth, a double row of fleshy lips open in a smile. Perhaps his throat has been brutally throttled; his guts bleed, concealing a shapeless mass of nitrous cream or rotting fat. With nimble fingers he can turn a sheet of crepe paper into a lily, a sparrow, or a light, iridescent hummingbird. For no magazine or newspaper or any kind of leaflet enters this hospital without being severely censored. The director only allows books and papers that deal with cheerful subjects, such as the handsome and arrogant Polyphemus, the deadly head of Gorgon, naughty fauns in love, ogres and witches, divine Pan, Lilliputians, sea creatures and their delicate women.

Jerico loves and is loved because of the happiness that radiates from him injecting in others a desire to live. His face lights up like an angel's, his body shines with the aqueous glitter of a starfish. With lively agility he moves from one bed to another as if on jumping pads. Is he young or old? Nobody knows. Jerico understands how to caress a fevered brow, to comfort the mass of beating flesh of a body anguished by ineffable earthly nostalgia, to sing to sleep the macrocephalic Siamese twins, spoon-feed the tender and pretty Ada. He even simulates tasty soups under Chief Balloon's direction.

And so it is. They all love Jerico, that archangel head like a Renaissance sculpture, those long blue curls, the voice that carries the sound of the wind and the faint rustle of crabs on the sand. His starlike nature forms the only link between the inmates of the ward and the exclusive areas of the outside world, where all of them would like to live.

Jerico moves rapidly. The special texture of his skin allows him to cling to the brick wall and reach the only window. How wonderful to be able to do that! And he loves to do it. His eyes of blue hydrangeas do not fall on the people walking on the beach, do not look at them. Not once has he said, "There goes the lifesaver, the blonde in the bikini, the balloon seller, the ice-cream van, a boat race . . ."

He has a way of telling and weaving his tales, and his listeners ride on the sound of his voice toward horizons beyond the window. He can easily spot the slender silhouette of a yacht outlined between the calm indigo sea and the fiery sunset, sailing into the night that quivers with thousands of liquid silver stars.

Jerico is so beautiful that it hurts to look at him. He knows how to rock the seagulls in the wind, to capture the faint reflection of flying fishes over the rippling, metallic phosphorescence of the waves; he forecasts the outrage of the imminent storm and lovingly counts the dolphins. Then, tired, he comes down to rest for a while. He still smells of the sea, of harbors, small bays, and coves; his wet hair carries particles of algae, the glowing of iodine, sand, chlorophyll. Everybody absorbs the revitalizing salt that clings to and impregnates the extremities of his body, ulcerated from the effort of leaning so long out the window.

Jerico is half the life of the hospital ward.

Jerico is the object of everybody's blind unconditional love. Nobody could imagine him being struck down by sudden melancholy after hearing him describe the Melusina circus parade.

He howled, screamed, whistled, and laughed until at times he ran out of breath. He was not allowed to clap at the splendid sight of the camels' fabled harnesses, or the ferocious Bengal tigers, the gentle llamas, the Arab mares, the red plumage and stylized steps of the Colombian horses, and the dappled giraffes nibbling green eucalyptus leaves. As for the dancing dogs, the saffron shine of the elephants, and the smooth copper manes of the fierce lions, the lights and bells and accordions, the cymbals, maracas, and flutes of burnished metal . . . and the cheery streamers and unimaginable sparkle and raining of the rockets and roman candles mixing in the liquid darkness of the night. And in the background the murmur of the waves forever breaking.

Too much emotion for Jerico. By the end of the night, he goes down with a high fever. His weak, displaced heart, the size of a dove's egg, fails him in his sleep. By dawn, death, like a wandering and wingless star, claims him and also kisses for the thousandth and last time the pure forehead of pretty Ada, thin as a needle.

Dead, Jerico resembles a beautiful bird, cursed and struck down by the plague. They do not bury him in a leafy garden as one does with a pet animal, or in the cemetery close to the hospital. Instead, he is secretly incinerated to avoid panic and suspicion. His death must not arouse attention in the outside world.

Jerico's ashes, scattered to the wind, will return particle by particle to the nurturing bosom of the earth, or gather into a new set of cells perhaps to form the body of a luckier man. The world that saw him born, the house that watched him grow with horror, will now remember him breathing with relief.

The inmates of the ward go on loving Jerico, passionately; they miss him but without pain. Death is another face of fortune, a small step on the way to real freedom, the only way possible for somebody like him, the accursed bird, archangel-star; a monster hidden inside his gleaming, wet nonhuman skin.

Or perhaps Jerico's soul has gone to the shining depths of the sea. Or is kneeling among the Seven Celestial Choirs. . . . If the others could sing, they would chant eternal hymns in his honor. In the ward nobody is trying to forget him. They cling step by step to their routine as the logical way to preserve their sanity. The nurses come three times a day to empty the pots full of urine and excrement and to check the oxygen dispensers, iv bags, and iron lungs. They are good, ordinary people. They rub the patients with methylated spirits, smiling kindly all the time, and help them cut their nails – if there are still any – eat their meals, and scrupulously change their dirty sheets.

Everything goes on normally in this world of abnormality. It is four weeks since Jerico's disappearance when a blond giant comes to take his place, with its disinfected bed and new covers. His name is Arsenio, but soon he is nicknamed the Slippery Lamppost. Even seated or kneeling he is taller than Gaston the Night. He sleeps all doubled up in the large bed that is reinforced with metal bars.

Arsenio's growth is uncontrollable. He has been shooting up for twenty years. To start with, whenever he went out, his very presence caused disturbance, turmoil, even accidents in the streets. Eventually, he stopped fighting against his cruel fate, became afraid of those he loved, and began to resent their sad embarrassed looks. Little by little he learned to face the hard task of for-getting.

Having taken Jerico's place, he has become one of the inmates. One evening Chief Balloon formally asks him, begs him, to go to the window.

"Just describe anything you like, truthfully. You don't have to give us the names of strange people."

Arsenio indolently navigates the way across the ward between the white beds and the repellent smells. Walking does not particu-larly hurt him, but his legs are as limp as a rag, his bones the pasty texture of soft wood. Not a trace of tension in his wobbly muscles. He is a bewildered, frightened youth brutally hit by life. From afar he could be taken for a tightrope walker made of badly assembled plastic. With weary eyes, pointed chin, and droopy jowls he con-fronts this new and limited universe.

Very, very slowly he approaches the window, his absurdly long curved back trembling. They watch him pucker his aquiline nose, press his rounded forehead against the frosted glass, and raise a large flat hand to pull the latch. In a loud and impatient voice, he says:

"There is nothing, absolutely nothing. Just a cement wall."

Bored and disappointed, twisting his long legs and knocking his knees, he returns to his bed.

Translated from the Spanish by Psiche Hughes

Young Amatista

The girls' mound of Venus is still almost bald, except for two or three hairs that have just sprouted. The hairs appeared on both Amatista and Mariolina at almost the same time, and they are very proud of them. Let's listen to the girls' conversation:

"Has your hair grown a lot, Mariolina?" Amatista asks.

"It's grown a lot and gotten curly, and I've got two more."

"Do you touch them often?"

"I go around touching them all day long. Whenever I can, I go somewhere private and look at them."

"Me too, Mariolina."

"Tell me, Amatista," says Mariolina, "do you like to squeeze your butt against the chair?"

"I love to, and after I've been sitting for a long time I get all tingly you-know-where and I have to squeeze even harder against the chair."

"And the harder you squeeze, the more you feel like squeezing, right?"

"Yes, Mariolina, I squeeze myself more and more until the little wave comes."

"I always get the little wave during last class period. The teacher is as sleepy as we are, so she doesn't notice anything."

"I get it when I go to tea parties with mama, and since I'm a big girl already, they make me sit with the ladies. But I don't take part in the conversation, so I just think about my cousin Hernán."

"Did he finally show it to you, like he said he would?"

"I'll tell you all about it. But first show me your hairs Amatista."

"To do that I'll have to take off my panties and go over by the candle where there's light. Don't forget, there's only candlelight in this room."

"Do it."

"What if mama comes in?"

"After you take off your panties, put them under your pillow. We'll go over to the bedside table, the one that's farthest from the door, and we'll cover ourselves up a little with the blankets, while you go over to the candelabrum. If you hear mama coming, we'll cover ourselves all up with the blankets and pretend to be sleeping."

"Okay"

"Do you want me to show you my hairs, too?"

"Sure. Let me help you take off your panties. Did you ever let your cousin put his fingers underneath, like he wanted to?"

"Yes, but that's all he did. Hernán is already a grown man, you know, and he might want . . . and I'm just a little girl."

"Of course. Let's see, Mariolina. What cute hairs! And they're already curly. Do you straighten them out?"

"Whenever I can."

"Help me take off my panties!"

"Sure. Come on, quick! Let's put our panties under the pillow. Your hairs are very pretty. Tell me Amatista, does yours get all wet?"

"Of course it does. It gets very slippery inside."

"Watch out, Amatista! I hear noises outside. Let's get under the blankets. Now I don't hear the noises anymore, but let's stay like this just in case."

"Okay. Listen Mariolina."

"Yes, Amatista? Oh! What are you doing?"

"I was going to ask you if I could touch you, but my finger got ahead of my question. Do you want to touch me, too?"

"Mama says I mustn't touch my little button."

"My mama says the same thing, but look, Mariolina, you're not touching it. I'm touching it, right?"

"You're so smart! So don't you ever touch yours?"

"How about you?"

"I never touch mine, Amatista."

"Then who touches it for you?"

"My cousin Hernán, ever since I let him put his finger under the edge of my panties last time."

"Tell me what it was like."

"Okay, but first let me find your button. Here it is. Mmm . . ."

"Okay, I'll tell you. It was Sunday, at noon, and we had just finished lunch here in the country house."

"Country house, but it's on a cobblestone street!"

"It's a cobblestone street in a one-horse town. The country starts right here, let's say right where the house ends."

"Yes, Mariolina."

"As I was saying, the whole family had just eaten lunch: my parents, my grandparents, and my aunt and uncle, Hernán's parents."

"And his little brothers and sisters?"

"Yes, his little brothers and sisters, too, the ones who are always spying through the keyhole, and also his deaf great aunt. It was a very hot day: the smell of hay coming in through the open windows of the dining room. Haystacks, you know. We could also hear the birds singing and the insects buzzing. Amatista, do you want to take your finger away from there while I tell you? I can't talk when I feel the little wave coming. Okay, I was saying that it was very hot; after they served ice cream, coffee, and after-dinner drinks, the men went into the parlor to smoke cigars, and the women went upstairs to take a siesta with the children. Hernán and I were the only ones left in the dining room, pretending to look at Dad's butterfly collection. While we were standing at the window, Hernán pinched me a few times on the rear end. Meanwhile, we could hear the men talking in the smoking room. When

I squatted down to show Hernán the big butterflies on the lowest shelf, he leaned toward me and grabbed my butt with both hands. You know it isn't easy to squeeze butt through our ruffled dresses and starched petticoats. At that moment the men must have left the smoking room to go up to their rooms, because we stopped hearing their voices."

"Hernán stopped looking at the butterflies," Mariolina said, "and he went to sit in the big armchair next to the grandfather clock. The house was totally quiet: everyone was in their bedrooms taking a siesta. Hernán called me over to sit on his lap."

"And did you?"

"Of course I did; I always do. Don't forget, Hernán is a few years older than me, and I've always been his dear little cousin. He was the first one to notice when I grew tits, no matter how small they were."

The two girls burst out laughing.

"Be quiet Amatista, I heard another noise outside," Mariolina said, squeezing Amatista's love button as if that were the way to keep her still.

"I don't hear anything, Mariolina," said Amatista, listening carefully and gently moving Mariolina's hand to ease the pressure. Mariolina left the inside of the tender rose and covered the outside with her whole hand as if she were hiding it from someone's gaze. And with her whole hand she began to make slow circular motions.

"What's that, Mariolina?" Amatista asked.

"Do you like it?" Mariolina asked.

"I don't want you to take your hand away, ever, Mariolina; don't stop doing what you're doing. Did Hernán teach you that, too?"

"No, Amatista, I taught it to him. That is, I taught him to do it to me. I learned it here, from one of the maids."

"I'm sure it was the cook's assistant who taught you."

"How did you know?" Mariolina asked, guiding Amatista's hand to imitate her own.

"Because she has milky white skin, with freckles on her cheeks and on her chest."

"Ah, yes. You know I never liked to take a siesta. When everyone in the house went to bed, I used to go to the kitchen to watch Juana (her name was Juana) mop the kitchen floor. I was little, Amatista, so I was very surprised when Juana, who was drying the floor with a rag, said to me, 'listen, child, I can see your panties from down here.' I shrugged my shoulders and was about to leave the kitchen when Juana said. 'Come here and I'll do something nice to you.' She put down the bucket and the rag and sat down in a chair. 'Come here,' she insisted. I didn't know what it was all about, but something made me go over to Juana, who had turned a little red and was panting. When she had me next to her, she put her hand underneath my skirt and grabbed me you-know-where with her whole hand, and she started to do what I'm doing to you now."

"But was it outside your panties?"

"Of course, and this way, too."

Mariolina's hand stopped making circular motions and started to move firmly up and down. Amatista imitated it with her own hand. The girls were silent for a while, until both of them decided to remove their hands to continue the story.

"And did you teach Hernán to do that to you?"

"Sure, it was convenient. I wasn't disobeying mama with that business about not touching my little button, and we could do it outside our clothing in case anyone came in. Do you hear anything?"

"I don't hear anything, Mariolina, and anyway we're in bed all covered up."

"But mama might get angry if she found us awake at this hour.

She thinks that nighttime is for sleeping. Okay, let's keep our voices low and no laughing. I sat on Hernán's lap, as usual, and he felt my tits to see if they had grown since the last time we were together. They hadn't grown much, but Hernán said it was a matter of patience."

"And then?"

"He put his hand under my skirt and gave me a squeeze you-know-where."

"That happened before, right?"

"Yes, but this time Hernán was acting different. He was panting by my ear and he asked me if I'd let him. I didn't know what he wanted me to let him do, but just in case, I said yes."

"And what did he do?"

"He put one finger under the edge of my panties, found my hairs, and congratulated me on them. He was still panting, and he touched me where mama said you mustn't. Oh, Amatista!"

"What?"

"You're rubbing my little button just like Hernán."

"Rub me too, and let the little wave come."

The girls fell silent, each with her finger moving over the love button of the other. Caressing and caressing, panting all the while, they brought about their little waves effortlessly, and immediately fell asleep. Outside the door, a noise could be heard, but the girls didn't hear it. It was the visitor who had been there all the time, spying through the keyhole, and jerking off so violently that he unwittingly knocked at the door. Frightened, the visitor – none other than Pierre, the stable boy, still an adolescent who hadn't yet met Amatista – did up his fly and ran off down the staircase, with the intention of getting out of the building as quickly as possible to continue masturbating in his corner of the stable.

Amatista and Mariolina slept like logs till next morning, when a sunbeam filtering through the window awakened them, along with the birds' singing and the noise from a water pump that the maid was using. Immediately they retrieved their underpants from beneath the pillow, put them on, and jumped out of bed to go wash their faces at the washbasin and get dressed.

"A washbasin, how strange," said Amatista.

"It was my grandmother's, and we keep it because it's so pretty," Mariolina explained.

While they slipped their dirndl-skirted dresses over their starched petticoats, Amatista asked:

"When will your cousin come back, Mariolina?"

"Next Sunday, Amatista."

"How nice! I'll be here. Mama said that we'll come next Sunday. Tell me, Mariolina, is it true that when you grow up you'll turn into a guy with a monocle?"

"That's completely false, Amatista. I'm going to turn into a beautiful woman, with divine tits and a thick, dark silky tangle on my mound of Venus. The one who is going to turn into a gentleman is my cousin."

"What a funny mistake! Let's go have breakfast, Mariolina."

One day Amatista was walking along absentmindedly, admiring the birds, fruit, and flowers, when the gentleman with the monocle grabbed her from behind, squeezing her breasts with his hands. Pierre, while masturbating, watched as Amatista stretched out on the grass in full sunlight and began to masturbate herself, perhaps acceding to a request by the monocled gentleman, who stood by watching her and masturbating without ever dropping his monocle. Afterward, Amatista and the gentleman lay down to enjoy a siesta by Pierre's side, beneath the gigantic tree. Amatista dreamed that she was surrounded by naked people. Although their bodies were all rather nice, they weren't perfect.

The young men carried a girl on a little golden chair that they supported with their crossed arms. The girl rested her hands on the youths' shoulders and rubbed her derrière against the palms of their hands. Her eyes were closed, her mouth open, and she was moaning softly. Another woman was teaching a young man to delay his ejaculation while masturbating. They sat face to face, and she herself moved his hand aside when she noticed his movements become more rapid. A few birds flew overhead, chirping. A girl swung from the branch of a tree, spreading her legs as she swung above the head of a young man who stood beneath the branch, brushing his tongue against the inside of her half open rose. Sundry groups of people tossed about gently in the grass, bumping against each other and squeezing a penis or a breast as they passed over one another, or else thrusting an exploratory finger into the fleshy petals of someone's moist rose.

It was nightfall. In her dream Amatista saw the monocled gentleman, whose usually stern expression became sweeter as he tossed his monocle up to the sky. Instead of describing a curve and falling, the monocle continued to ascend, landing on a pink cloud where an angel played the harp, entangling his erect penis among the strings.

"This will come in handy!" exclaimed the angel as he grabbed the monocle in flight. "I'm so nearsighted that I can never tell if I'm touching a string of the harp or my own penis, and some of my sensations are hardly celestial!"

"Don't be afraid," answered a keen-sighted angel from another cloud. "All the parts of our bodies were created by the Almighty and are therefore a miracle. Just consider: isn't it a miracle that this thing, which was so floppy and small before, has suddenly grown and become stiff like this?"

The angel whose penis was entangled in the strings of the harp suddenly felt his penis jerk loose abruptly, but not without first making the instrument vibrate as powerfully as pealing bells. All the angels in heaven came to attention and prepared to hear the words of the Almighty.

From the highest cloud, the Almighty, who (understandably)

was draped in a white toga, began to speak with a harmonious, warm, and peaceful voice. "My children," the Almighty began, "I am about to reveal unto you my New Law."

There was a murmur among the angels and humans, and then total silence.

"First Commandment," said the Almighty. "Though shalt know and explore thy body. Thou shalt fondle thy flesh and caress the pubic hair and all parts of the body, especially the genitalia. Second Commandment: thou shalt learn to use thy tongue, fingers, genitalia and every part of thy body to caress the bodies of others. Third Commandment: thou shalt masturbate as often as thou wilt, alone or accompanied. Fourth Commandment: thou shalt try all the positions and all the mischief of pleasure, and thou shalt invent games like a child. . . ."

A joyous chorus interrupted the pronouncement of the New Law. The Almighty smiled and lifted his toga, displaying his erect penis. An angel approached with a bunch of dark grapes, recently washed in celestial springs, and rubbed them several times against the phallus of the Almighty, who at last spilled his divine seed on the grapes. A happy noise rose up from the multitude of angels and humans, and the gentleman who had launched his monocle up to heaven caught it smack on the head as it was returned to him.

When Amatista awakened it was already night. She, Pierre, and the monocled gentleman started back toward the house in the poplar grove, as it was time to dress for dinner.

Translated from the Spanish by Andrea G. Labinger

Farewell, My Love

Three vowels, one *r*, and one *l* left; it must be possible to find a seven-letter word and win the game. All she has to do is to take another sip of coffee and concentrate for a few minutes, moving the letters around on the stand, and there it is: *warbler*. Seven letters, fifty bonus points, sixty-four total.

"Already getting rid of all your letters?" Pablo says. "Can't you see it's giving me a chance of a triple-letter score?"

"How so? What can you put down? *Warblerize*?"

While he is thinking hard about the next move, twisting the ends of his moustache, she looks intently at the board to avoid looking at him. Yet she can't help but see his lowered face and realize how painful it will be not to see it anymore. How she will miss the weight of his body. Three wasted years, as her grandmother would say, he wasted three years of your life.

"I can't think of anything," Pablo says after a while. "All I can make is *it* and get three points."

"You have an *f*, why don't you add to *it*, make *fit* and then *for* across. You get a double score and a total of seventeen points."

"You've been looking at my letters again."

"I do it to help you, otherwise the game becomes very boring," says Laura. And though she realizes that it will put a stop to the game, she adds impulsively:

"You've met somebody."

"Yes," says Pablo, surprised and relieved at the same time. "How do you know?"

"*Mutilate*, I get rid of all my letters again," says Laura, proud of having once again found such a good word for her *u* and *a* using another vowel from the board.

Proud and shattered. Thinking of winning an imaginary game with *shatter*, placing *h* on a triple-letter score and then, with luck, picking the necessary *e* and *d* before her opponent to make *shattered* and getting the triple-word score.

It would be enough to beat a much better player than Pablo. She writes down the score for *mutilate*, even though she senses that to go on playing no longer has any meaning.

"I'm not sure. I just know. I can tell. You saw her last night," she adds guessing, "but you haven't slept together yet."

"Clever bitch! You know everything," Pablo says with some admiration.

Laura does not know everything, but she is beginning to understand. All the muscles of her body seem to slacken, lose their strength. Will she be able to stand up? She lights a cigarette. Her movements are slow as if she were under water, deeply under, with all the weight of the ocean on top. And she feels cold. To escape from the pain, she tries to imagine herself a year from now, with another man, thinking back with indifference about the present situation.

Love is like a hippopotamus, trotting clumsily through the forest, devastating entire sections as it advances, indifferent to anything except gathering food and splashing in the water. Stupid, bungling love.

"So you won't want to see me again. It's all over."

"Yes, all over." Pablo doesn't want to look at her; but he's happy that her intuition has saved him so many difficult explanations, and now he looks at her with tenderness, caressing her face.

"I love you, you know this as well, don't you?"

This is the last straw. Pablo's affection, good opinion, and appreciation is more than she can bear. Laura thinks of all that is lacking in his "I love you" and knows she can't live with that kind of love, and she doesn't want to be remembered that way, with gentle affection.

"Now that it's all over, we can tell each other the truth, can't we? You can tell me who you were with last weekend when you went to Mendoza. I'm curious."

"I've already told you that nothing happened when I went to Mendoza for the conference."

"What game are you playing? It doesn't matter any more. I know that you were with somebody. It showed."

"Okay. I didn't go to Mendoza, I went to see one of my cousins from Córdoba. Do you remember her?"

"And I was with Panchito. Last weekend I was with Panchito."

"Why did you do that?" says Pablo, not quite believing what he's heard, yet already suffering, anguished, pale, as if he had just received a hard blow on his head. After all, Laura loved him and had never minded his little infidelities, as long as he came back, while he, who does not love her, was driven mad with pain and jealousy at her infidelities.

"You don't think I was going to stay at home sucking my thumb while you went about deflowering your young cousins?"

This time the allusion is not random: it refers to one of Pablo's weaknesses. Uncertain of his sexual attraction, he is inclined to seek the challenge, the more difficult, daunting task of seducing a virgin. Once, one of his students gave him, as a sign of her gratitude, a leather-bound copy of *Martín Fierro*. Pablo showed it to Laura with some embarrassment.

"But I didn't ask you anything," says Pablo. "I don't want to know anything. Why did you have to come and tell me this?"

Laura is not clear why: she's looking for a way to hurt him, something that will make him feel part of her pain. She imagines piercing his chest with a long thin instrument, a knitting needle, or one of those with a hook on the end. And then tearing it out and dabbing the wound with mustard.

"We had good fun, Panchito and I. I've been wanting to for some time."

During the last three years, Laurita has come to know Pablo very well and understands that, even if the tune of love may be broken, she can still make him dance to the rhythm of hatred. This is going to be strong and hearty, a damn good kind of farewell.

"And what did you do?" says Pablo, feigning indifference.

"What did we do? We made love."

"How many times?"

"What does it matter?"

"I've asked you, how many times?" Pablo's restrained voice hisses now, though still impersonal and remote.

"Three times."

"And then, did you sleep with him again?"

"No, you came back from Mendoza then, or rather from Córdoba. I haven't seen him since."

"And how does Panchito fuck? Better than me?"

"I don't know. Different. You don't want to know the details, do you?"

Pablo drops all appearances of calm, cold, scientific curiosity and moves heavily toward her. His eyes look bloodshot, and he is panting, trembling with hatred and jealousy.

Laurita pushes against the back of the armchair.

Pablo grabs her arm and squeezes her wrist tightly.

"Indeed, I do, you dirty little hooker, you worn-out old broad. You are going to tell me all the details. Did you suck him? I want to know all. Answer me. You are going to tell me whether you gave him a blow job."

"Yes I did, let me go." Laurita is twisting with pain and trying to free her arm.

Pablo asks how she sucked him; did she put it all in her mouth, caressing it with her tongue? Did he come in her mouth?

Laura does not want to answer, but Pablo accompanies each of his questions with a hard, sharp slap, until she begins to taste blood in her mouth.

Finally Laura, with an explosion of anger, pain, and desire, begins to invent, basing her story on the vague memory of a brief episode, a year ago. An episode to be treasured and remembered as something to talk about in the future because, even though she had liked the idea, Laura only slept with Panchito because of Pablo. And now with pleasure she tells Pablo how she slowly licked first his balls, then from the base up to the tip, slowly, until finally she took it all into her mouth and started a measured sucking movement, still working with her tongue. Until Panchito came and she felt the sourish warm taste of his semen. And she swallowed it, which is a lie, because Laurita does not like the taste, it makes her retch, and Pablo ought to know, to remember this, if only he were in a condition to know and remember anything.

"And what's Panchito's rod like? Is it big, bigger than mine?"

"Panchito does not have a rod, he has a saber. Longer than yours, and thinner, slightly bent at the end. That's why he doesn't call it a rod as you call yours, he calls it his saber – the hooked saber of General San Martín."

And now openly enjoying the situation and without the need for slaps, Laurita hits back by indulging in the detailed description and classification of the men she had met or imagined. How they all happened to give a particular name to their sex, invented or chosen, among the many known names. And how such a name is generally associated with certain physical characteristics that they consider universal but are in fact very private and personal. So Laurita has met with a "Bean Pod," a "Big Head," a "Magic Wand," a "Jack-on-a-Beanstalk," a "Police Truncheon." And with delight she now describes the range of different pleasures – decidedly imaginary – that each tool can provoke in a woman according to its shape and size.

Now Pablo wants to silence her and, coiling his hand in her hair, drags her down, twisting her arm, and at the same time forcing her on to her knees, with her head thrown back. He has undone his trousers and makes Laurita suck him, Pablo. Just like she sucked Panchito.

Next he, Pablo, makes her, Laurita, turn around, take her shirt off, and caress her breasts. He looks at her, half biting the ends of his moustache while she caresses herself, and helps her take off her trousers and forces her to move across the room, half naked on all fours.

Laurita obeys, comes running like a little dog, and he kisses her neck, playfully bringing his mouth to her nipples and withdrawing it, hardly touching them with his lips and moustache. Then, placing his mouth on one nipple, he skillfully brushes it with his teeth, while he surrounds her waist with his arms, caressing her hips and buttocks. Slowly, the other hand moves upward from one knee along the inner side of her thighs to the center; fingers dip in her damp sex, lubricating his frighteningly tender caress.

Waves of desire surge from inside Laurita, turn into convulsive spasms; desire, too, is pleasure, desire and pleasure knotted together. It prickles her as if an incredibly fine needle entered the tips of her fingers. Now she can't resist it any longer and moans through her half-open mouth; the sound of excited pleasure, her own breathing turned into a voice that raises even more the wave of her desire.

Now Pablo enters her, his tongue in Laura's mouth, going round her teeth and gums, forcing her to open her tightened jaws, raping her mouth as he moves inside her body. He calls her "my mare," "my whore" and shuddering together both reach the final interminable moment.

A little later all gets back to normal, and Pablo is tenderly caressing Laurita's hair. As they dress, they remember with some sadness that they were about to part, and she, Laurita, begins to weep, and Pablo also weeps, a little. Then they embrace very tightly, and Pablo asks Laurita's forgiveness for not loving her any more, and Laurita wonders why on earth he has stopped loving her, the mysteries of love, that bungling hippopotamus.

Pablo is leaving, this time forever. While they are waiting for the escalator on the landing, he looks at Laura with affection. "You're a good girl. I'm going to miss you."

At this point, Laura stands on tiptoes and makes Pablo bend down: there's something she wants to say in his ear. With her arms around Pablo, Laurita whispers in his ear,

"You never asked: Panchito gave it to me in the arse as well." She then re-enters her apartment and shuts the door. She drags herself to the bathroom like the tired, beaten boxer who returns to the dressing room still hearing the cries that celebrate the winner. Her face is like that of the beaten boxer – worse perhaps: stained with blood, semen, snot, sweat, and tears black with mascara. Soaping herself under the shower, letting the water soak her hair and run along her body, Laurita thinks that Pablo can hit and humiliate her, seduce her, give her pleasure, pain, and sadness, can abandon her, but never, never in a million years can Pablo beat Laurita at Scrabble.

Translated from the Spanish by Psiche Hughes

Immensely Eunice

1

Eunice was twenty-seven and weighed three hundred pounds. Only a century ago a painter would have employed her as a model, and she could have earned her living by it. These days, however, she had been looking for work over a period of many long useless months, during which the old fridge was opened with increasing frequency.

It is generally estimated that fat people watch television on average eleven hours a day. And assumed that, on top of that, fat women read large numbers of romantic magazines. Eunice, however, didn't even glance at them. She rarely tasted a potato chip, even less so with her eyes fixed on the luminous screen.

At the time she was looking for work, no food shop was prepared to take her on for fear that she would secretly eat everything within her reach. Eunice finally did find employment in a flower shop. Nobody could imagine that she might want to taste the ferns and the geraniums or savor the yellow roses. On the other hand, she was well acquainted with the names of flowers and, from the aura of candor that emanated from her round face, the shopkeeper guessed that her large presence would suit the place well.

Eunice spent hours there sitting on a wooden stool. The tape recorder played a cassette of new-age music over and over. At times Eunice stretched her puffy hand to caress the leaves of a poinsettia, feeling the roughness with the tips of her fingers. Immensely, time slipped away.

2

Eunice lived in an old apartment in the Calle San José. Eunice spent Sundays lying on her bed; her flesh equally distributed on both sides, right and left and in close connection with the mat-

57

tress, she let herself be carried away by the sounds that emerged from the gray stairwell of the building. Sounds that seemed to come from the open mouth of a Carthaginian god; children's cries; women rushing to prepare lunch; shots emitted from an American soap opera; badly tuned radios; men arguing.

In spite of her hundred and fourteen kilos, Eunice never did any cooking. Every Saturday, after closing the shop, she went to a crowded market that zigzagged along the edge of her barrio. Carrying large bags, she stopped in front of the cold-meats truck towering above the heads of waiting customers with a mixture of products that hung in front of their eager eyes: clusters of rosy chorizos, endless circles of blood puddings with African skin, aging salamis, sausages gleaming with fat, the ribcage of some animal now lost forever, and occasionally the sleepy head of a piglet with very sad ears.

Waiting her turn, Eunice ran her eyes along the great mass of pork destined to become human meat. She bought a good assortment of mortadela and other kinds of bologna, a pig's head, topside, and long chipolata sausages, and – if available – a magnificent aromatic pâté.

Then with one bag filled, Eunice turned to the cheese stall and there, as the numbers were called, she became engrossed in the Gruyère's maze of holes, the amusing sight of moldy Roquefort, and the varying tonalities, from yellow to orange, of the fresh local cheeses, their names evoking green pastures and a farmer's family up at sunrise.

Eunice bought two pounds of butter, two pounds of *dulce de leche*, and two of plum jam. She watched the gooey contents of the large jars emptying out, the reluctant sugary remains sticking together.

After visiting these stalls, all that was left was a routine call at the baker's. There she bought various loaves, homemade bread in the shape of mythological horns freshly out of the oven, and several cartons of milk.

Heavily weighed down, Eunice returned home slowly, as the lofty images of Saturday evening and Sunday rose in front of her eyes. A half-read biography of some martyr, some hero, a traveler, or a musician inevitably waited on the little table by the side of her massive bed.

3

There were two types of clients in her shop: those in love with plants, and those in love with someone. These varied considerably in their range: fiancés, lovers, intimate best friends, sons of widowed mothers. But they never hung about. On the other hand, those who came to look for a specific plant took their time. With scientific skill they scrutinized the green of the leaves, the dampness of the soil, the smell.

A blind man stood out among them. He wore dark glasses, which he never took off, and Eunice sensed that something unspeakable was hidden behind those lenses. He was a connoisseur of the vegetable world and, before he bought a plant, carefully considered questions of light, humidity, location, and pruning. He spoke little, and Eunice watched how he walked around the shop without asking questions, identifying each leaf with his fingers and stretching out his hand to measure the height of a shrub.

Eunice struggled within herself between wanting to know whether the blind man was able to visualize the color of the plants – either by imagining it or by remembering it from a time past, before darkness flooded his world – and keeping the respectful silence of a fat person who prefers breathing slowly to engaging her clients in eager conversation.

The blind man always smelled the flowers on display and identified them. He was never wrong. Eunice smiled at his correct guesses but did not allow herself to laugh outright. She was afraid that he might notice the breathlessness that goes with obesity. Every time she saw him coming, Eunice immediately took a bottle of eau de cologne from a drawer to freshen up her neck and arms. A man with such a sharp sense of smell could perceive the aromatic traces of three hundred pounds, even among so much beauty.

4

One day the blind man asked Eunice to do a job for him on a Sunday. She had to prune the creepers on his garden walls that threatened to invade the windows of the neighboring house. Although he loved gardening, that job was beyond him. He promised she would have the use of a ladder to climb up the walls. Eunice accepted but was terrified: what if she broke the ladder and came crashing down in front of the bewildered blind man as he attempted to lift her immense, bruised body?

Accordingly, the following Sunday, she made her way to the house of the blind man in a state of great alarm. It was a beautiful small building in Bello y Reboratti, next to the Rodo Park. Inside, by the gate, there was a handsome wooden spiral staircase, which led to the upper floor. Eunice sighed with relief when the blind man suggested they go out into the garden by the other side. With luck the old oak stairs would not creak under her weight. The thoughtful man had everything ready in the garden – clippers, gardening gloves, a hose, and other equipment – all laid out by a robust metal ladder, the kind sold in ironmonger and hardware shops. This filled Eunice with confidence, and she started working in earnest.

5

By the afternoon Eunice and the blind man had arranged the enormous creepers and the branches of bougainvillea. In August that year the weather was almost summery; by the end of the day Eunice was caked in sweat, soil, and dust. The twilight was approaching, and the blind man suggested she take a shower in the bathroom on the ground floor next to the kitchen. With obliging rapidity he brought large white towels with initials embroidered in italics. Eunice was exhausted, though lighthearted and happy, and accepted without thinking too much about it. She bolted the door, took off her working clothes and, after looking at herself for a while in the mirror, went under the steaming shower. A warm sense of well-being overcame her, and she started humming a song above the din of the running water. She shut her eyes under the jets that gushed over the back of her head as the rushing water exploded against the porcelain.

Suddenly, her hum turned to a scream. Two strange hands, eager and persistent, were feeling their way around Eunice's enormous body under the shower. How could it be? She trembled. Then she understood. True to the layout of old houses, the bathroom had two doors. One of them had been left unlocked.

Terror paralyzed Eunice. The blind man, soaking under the shower and fumbling with both hands, was discovering with surprise the full size of her body – her thighs, her protruding belly, the rolls under her armpits, her supernatural breasts, her immense fatness.

The water ran over his dark lenses, but he did not interrupt his holy task: with dedication he completed a detailed survey of Eunice's body, while outside night was gaining over the twilight.

6

Every Sunday during the following six months, Eunice arrived at the house of the blind man to work in his garden. In the summer, the jasmine burst with perfume, the rosebushes trailing up the wall were getting redder by the day, and the old magnolia tree in the center of the garden seemed to dominate the air surrounding the city.

Eunice was no longer afraid of the old oak staircase creaking. Having filled the house with sweet-scented branches, she and the blind man would climb up to the large bedroom on the top floor. There, in the center, stood a bed of dark cedar wood, and the rolls of Eunice's shoulders leaned evenly against its solid back, while the blind man rested, burying his face between her gigantic breasts.

At five in the afternoon the bell rang. It was the pâtissier, Esmeraldo, delivering the order that the blind man placed every Sunday. An assortment of divine sandwiches, nibbles of palm hearts with Roquefort and nuts, morsels of cheese and morello cherries, little baskets of artichoke hearts with Thousand Island sauce, cases of mayonnaise and olives, rolls of ham wrapped in angel-hair pasta, steaming croquettes of cheese and bacon, pastries and canapé filled with tuna, and, to finish, a magnificent tray of small cakes filled with chocolate or zabaglione, tarts with berries, pineapple and kiwi, truffles, millefeuilles, éclairs of *dulce de leche*, and jellies.

Eunice ate and caressed the forehead of the blind man, who no longer used his dark glasses, exposing the sight of his washed-out symmetrical pupils. They did not speak much.

7

One Sunday evening, as Eunice was about to shake her enormous body out of the bed and get dressed, the blind man announced that, in a fortnight's time, he would leave for Cuba. Eunice's immense heart stood still, and she remained speechless. The blind man filled her silence by explaining that he would receive treatment there and a series of operations over a period of four months, after which he might possibly recover his sight. There was a 60 percent chance of success, he said, and smiled, full of hope.

Eunice spoke favorably of the project, praised the blind man's enthusiasm, encouraged him, and encircled him in her splendid arms. But within her breast, under the many layers of fat, her heart shrank to the size of a little chick.

When they parted in the Moorish lobby of his house in Bello y Reboratti, the blind man could not see the tears that ran down her face. The door closed with a loud creak, and Eunice cursed her destiny, which was once more so cruel to her. Slowly, like a hundred-year-old turtle, she made her way home along the side of the lake in Rodo Park.

In a few months, she thought, the man who had just been embracing her would be able to see her as she was, fat and grotesque. Her gigantic deformed body would overflow the field of his newly restored sight.

8

The day after the blind man left for Cuba accompanied by an elderly aunt, Eunice's three hundred pounds headed for a slimming clinic. All the savings she had accumulated since starting work in the flower shop went to pay for treatment. The staff at the clinic assured her that she would soon start losing over twenty pounds a month. Besides suffering the rigors of an unspeakable diet, Eunice was to sip water throughout the day and walk numbers of miles between sunrise and the shop's opening time. In the evenings she was to go to a gym where a series of machines were to be found and sweaty people persistently engrossed in maneuvering them.

Underneath her lycra suit she had to wrap her large thighs, hips, and stomach in nylon to perspire even more and without relief.

Twice a day the slimming clinic sent her packets of food, its calories carefully calculated and any trace of salt, oil, and flour eliminated.

Every week a doctor with a face like a hamster examined Eunice, listened to her heart, inspected her eyes, and asked her routine questions. Though all the customers at the shop asked her with great concern if she was not feeling well, the doctor with a face like a hamster assured her that the treatment was progressing with excellent results.

On Saturday and Sunday Eunice did her exercises in front of the wardrobe mirror, resting every half hour for fifteen minutes on her old bed. In pants and bra she watched and felt her body. She stretched the palms of her hands over her buttocks and stomach and noticed the silent, secret metamorphosis that she was undergoing: the flight of her body toward regions of a lost past.

After three and a half months, Eunice could lie in bed on her side and see her hip bone sticking out; for so many years it had been out of sight, buried under layers of fat.

She noticed that now, in the streets, nobody looked astounded by her. One day she went to a boutique and bought herself a pair of normal-sized trousers. Running for the bus she managed to keep it waiting and got on it before it started off. Inside, other passengers could sit beside her now without feeling disturbingly uncomfortable.

9

One evening the phone in the shop rang and Eunice recognized the voice of the blind man telling her that he was no longer blind and that during the last six months the grass in the garden had grown out of control, the plants needed fertilizing, and there was weeding to be done. Trembling, Eunice arranged to see him at his house, as in the past.

It was autumn, and that Sunday Eunice did not wear her work clothes but a light dress of white cotton that hardly reached her knees. When she raised her small hand to ring the bell, the image of her chubby fingers doing the same only a year ago sprang before her eyes.

He opened the door: a pair of shining brown pupils fixed intently on her. He said nothing, waiting for her to say who she was. Pale and trembling, she smiled for a few seconds and then explained: she was Eunice, the very same Eunice who, while waiting for him to return, had decided to go on a diet. Her voice had lost the breathlessness that came from the pressure of so much fatty tissue and rang out in tune with the birds in Rodo Park.

The man who had been blind for sixteen years scrutinized her, and a shadow of disappointment shot across his face. Motionless, he could not bring himself to invite her in. It was only out of pure courtesy that he finally did so.

Translated from the Spanish by Psiche Hughes

Golden Days of a Queen of Diamonds

The being-with is a secret being-against
behind the mask of a being-for.

HEIDEGGER

Soon the euphoria will start. The sofa. I will lie down on the sofa of brilliant gold satin and wait. That's all I can do: wait and see what happens. Slowly I shall reach the full state of euphoria. Slowly. "Piano, pianissimo!" shrieks Miss Aurora Crane, wading bird, nesting on one leg in the middle of the scales. And grandfather fumes with anger behind the beveled glass partition on which, outlined in a golden web, enormous herons dream. He is fuming because he cannot stand Miss Aurora: worse than incompetent, she is extremely ugly. Bony and withered. And shortsighted, too. The old man kept his sense of aesthetics till his dying days; whenever the offensive presence of some ugly object or person assailed him, his nostrils would start to quiver in tempo and his eyebrows would arch. "Why don't you hire a decent-looking teacher?" he asked my mother reproachfully. "She is cheap." "But she looks awful and, besides, doesn't know how to teach. The child is not learning and has to listen to her hysterical squawking." "I'm not rich. If you pay the fees, I'll send her to the conservatory." "Don't make her take piano lessons if you can't afford a good teacher." "It's a must. All society girls take lessons."

Pianissimo. Soft, golden vapors in the evening sky. The launch advances lazily up the Santa Lucia. From the railings I look at the water that, at this point in the river, stinks. A lifeless, thick, almost congealed surface from which a breath of smelly soporific fumes arises. Esteban approaches from behind and presses himself to me. I feel his member level with my hip: pointed, hostile. But nothing else. Not even a tingle in my nerves. I feel his breath on my neck and hear him saying, "You have a beauty mark behind your right ear." He runs his tongue over the mole and wets my skin. "It's small and dark . . ." "Is that so?" "Didn't you know?" "I don't look behind my ears." Silly answer, I know, and cynical. Yet he is happy with it, happy with his discovery in the topography of my body. He makes me turn around: his reddish face shines, blue eyes, a thin moustache, golden like the edge of the clouds floating in the sky. A real archangel, Esteban. Esteban Peacock, high plumage, a tough beak, powerful and pointed. He is looking at me and imagines heavenly raptures, as if he thinks I'm still a virgin. He needs me to be a virgin to take me to the cabin of his motorboat, rush to my body, jump on top of it, all his strength let loose, and consummate his love in one, two, three, five strategic movements, rocked by the rolling complicity of the boat that, in its turn, assails the river. And thus feel in complete possession of me, unbeatable. Pity I am not a virgin, as he knows. That I have two children – one blond – and a husband – dark with a thick beard and the glasses of an intellectual, a lawyer – whose friend he is. "She is the wife of Doctor Falcon Clever-Lynx," they gravely told him, pointing at me one day as he was sitting in the office waiting room. I was calling on my husband, one of the most eminent figures in Montevideo, as witnessed by his prestigious surname. He has the sharp look of a lynx, can pierce a wall. Mr. . . . know-it-all. All the events of life are filed in an orderly way by his infallible beak. Because that's what he is: a unique specimen of falcon with a great future and a genealogy that, on his father's side, goes back to the tyrannosaurs of the antediluvian age. I stopped by to ask for money, as usual. To give me money was his main obligation. To ask for it my acquired right. More and more money to drown myself constantly in a sea of red, blue, and yellow banknotes. "Something you fancy, Laura?" "A magnificent diamond necklace, Alberto. It takes up the main window in the jewelers. All the women walking along Sarandi stop to admire it. I tried it on: it sparkles against my skin, covering it with shades of brilliant gold." "How much, darling?" "Not sure. I imagine between fifty and sixty thousand." It has to be a check, of course; his powerful hand, always in control, with dark hair over the fingers and the golden ring – a thick wedding ring. "Ask him for a thick ring, my child, and engraved, make the best of it, that's what his money is for." "But mother, wedding bands are meant to be simple." "Don't be silly, and ask him for a solitaire. You are beautiful and he is made of gold and crazy about you." And if I tried a gesture of protest: "It's him who makes a good marriage!" "Yes, mother, yes, mother." Daughter of a bitch. Your mother's daughter. She's a carnivorous, wide-arsed skunk. Never chase her, she knows how to defend herself. When cornered, she spurts out a long jet of pestiferous urine, by which she assaults and blinds the brave attacker and finally devours him. Your mother's daughter. You can't hide this from yourself. . . . "Yes, mother, yes, mother." As if it were all her fault. As if she had forced you to get married, poor docile little daughter; as if you didn't know, yes you, what you were in for. I am a bigger bitch than my mother and all under an angelic guise, an attitude of innocence, eyes shaded under the veil of illusions – for I did wear the veil – because the fashion is that virgins cover their face – and the fresh orange blossoms, and the sumptuous lace. How she bellowed, my mother, the big skunk, and sighed and said over and over again, "The sacrifices one makes for one's children." Because I was still unmarried and money was short, and the custom is that the bride's family pays for the wedding dress; it is the proper thing to do, even if the bride's family lives in well-disguised poverty, and "the lace is five hundred pesos a yard; all the same I will buy it, even if I have to pawn my

dead mother's diamond brooch. . . ." Cunning old vixen, you knew
perfectly well that you were going to get your money back – and
with interest. That's why you took me muttering, "What a shame"
and "God forgive me" and "Just as well my father is dead because
he would be so upset, so upset . . ." to Doctor Crush-Bones, terri-
fying bird of prey from the Caucasian mountains: a sweet smile,
sharp nails, talons held back. Yet how tender when she says to
me with the most moving expression of a professional hymen
mender, "It's not going to hurt you at all, my dear. I fix up to
a dozen girls a day, and you wouldn't believe how beautiful they
look only twenty-four hours later in church." The cathedral . . .
A very classy marriage. My mother, and my mother-in-law, old
magpies, birds of ill omen. I can still see them: one, blue feathers
on her toque – she decided on plumage, nothing less than bird of
paradise, and she paid a hundred dollars for it, although she was
a hundred years old. Ugly crooked fish – distinctive feature: a
twisted mouth. She felt she could wear feathers because she would
carry them over her head, and they weren't feathers but dollars.
My mother – mutter, mutter – chose the discreet adornment of
an ostrich tail. "My poor father," she explained, "died only four
months ago, and I will not wear a single touch of color out of
respect for him." I half close my eyes before starting my triumphal
entrance over the purple carpet: the first chords of the march have
already begun. I half close my eyes to face the truth of this holy
recess. I am entering it, on this occasion, as its central character,
the royal heron for once, in a pen of clucking birds waiting impa-
tiently, all in their feathers. Or rather a zoo, all in furs, and the men
dressed up like penguins. Facing me, Christ shines on his cross,
indifferent. As I advance, I notice his loathsome yellow face, the
insignificant terracotta countenance of the corpse; the absurdity
of this bloody sacrifice for the sake of men – and where are they? –
the ambivalent image of those lacquered drops of blood. The cru-
cified Christ bleeds over six rows of candles because, for such a

classy marriage, the whole crypt must be lit. After all, the family of
the groom paid for this and made a generous offering as set down
by the old and venerated tradition of the Catholic and Apostolic
Church of Rome. I advance on my father's arm and he, of course,
repeats the instructions of the maternal skunk: "Piano, pianissimo, the bride must take enough time to show herself off." I open
wide my pupils and smile, lightly, chastely under my veil of illu-
sion – with no illusions. And suddenly – I'm so inclined toward
elaborate tragic situations, even at moments like this – I think
that the magic stitching might pop open just now and start gently
dripping blood from the renewed hymen onto the oh-so-wonder-
ful lace. A thread of blood running along all five yards of the satin
train. What a terribly humiliating accident it would be, such a
sudden, irreverent flow. . . . My poor mother, my poor elder sister,
Hilda the Stork, wrapped in her cape of local fox, because "she
is not as pretty as Laura, what to do?" She just managed a decor-
ous match: she landed a good young man, the manager of a general store, but nothing more. Poor ashamed relatives, cockatoos
stopped in full glorious flight. Of course, nothing like this will
happen. I only felt a few twinges after the anesthetic wore off and
a few drops of blood on the cotton pad when I got back home.
After that, nothing. Alberto is waiting for me at the altar. I feel the
touch of his sweaty hand. He always sweats when he is nervous,
and how could he not be on his wedding day? But he was sweaty
also when he pressed me against the sofa and fondled my breast:
he held me tight and mother – lying low – dissimulated her presence until the moment when she would silently signal "Danger!"
and send my half-paralyzed grandfather in, dragging his suffering body and waddling like a seal as far as the screen of dreaming
herons. We'd see his shadow; Alberto sighed and the old man, following strict instructions, bent over coughing. We'd see his shaky
puppet shadow and Alberto would go back to caressing my hand
discreetly or, at most, my cheeks or my neck. Yet even if nobody

had watched us you would have never dared, Alberto, miserable Alberto, son of a bitch, son of your parents. Up to the last, you wanted to keep your role of the Proper Fiancé, fiancé up to the wedding night when, subtly disguising your brutality, you turned by right and by force, thanks to a single triumphant push, into the Great Falcon male. For Clever-Lynx knows that he needn't worry about the girl who is going to be his Respectable Wife, and that he can take his fire to the whorehouse, leaving the fiancée to find solace alone in the silent reserve of her virginal bed, chaste refuge for the night, whilst he assails unknown and nameless flesh and discharges into some warm hole the wicked product of his amorous passion so well restrained. That's all he needs.

My problems are starting . . . dryness, overall inflammation of the skin. My eyelids are burning, my eyes heavy like balls of lead. Whiskey will help. Two or three ice cubes clink happily as they lightly sink in the golden liquor. . . . "Esteban Peacock at your service." "He's the young architect I mentioned, Laura. He's going to make the plans for the holiday house on the island of Santa Lucia. On the little island my father left me, do you remember? A real paradise." Esteban. . . . Attractive smile under the golden moustache. My first lover. Blond, or some shade of blond, like the other three. Four years of marriage and four golden lovers, golden like my happy days. "I can take you on my motor launch, if you like, to see other chalets I have built on the delta. It's a lovely trip." His voice and eyes full of promise. I went once, twice, six times. The construction of the house on the island – bought in a whimsical attack of boredom by my defunct and well-remembered father-in-law, member of the long-lasting, illustrious breeds of Tyrannosaurs and antediluvian Unicorns, who nevertheless had made careful calculations ("land never loses its value, never") – was being infinitely postponed. Yet nothing happened. Not once did I get pleasure from Esteban. I am frigid – not true. Sensitive but incapable of making contact with the rest of the world. Why do you lie, Laura? You are still trying to make excuses. With what kind of shitty people could you have made contact, old, well-connected pieces of polychromatic mosaic, glued behind the color screen: "Move the kaleidoscope, child," grandfather used to say, "and flowers will appear, hearts, emeralds, rubies." But I only saw grandfather's creepy crawly eyes and rhinoceros horns. I didn't tell him of my failure. What was blond and handsome Esteban Peacock likely to understand, all absorbed with himself, with his flighty buildings on the shores of the river and his moustache of golden hairs? How could he touch this protective shell of shining, multishaped scales that was beginning to form over my glossy skin, shining hard and cold like a skin of diamonds? Who will find the silent burning embers that could be hidden under it, and what hand can draw the scalpel to cut and penetrate it down to the bone? He never asked any questions. Only once: if he would be able to interlock as a humble cog within the great mechanism that generations of Clever-Lynx had constructed one and a half centuries ago: "Not easy, Esteban, for a Peacock to enter the cage of a falcon without problems. You'd be destroyed. Not even if you had the daring to make away with his female. Not even then would you escape from his iron beak." He didn't appreciate the joke. They called him Estebanito at home. Pride and glory of his widowed mother. My archangel.

The ice sparkles through the glass – icebergs in a transparent sea. . . . Mirrors . . . always mirrors around, throwing back at me my positions and gestures . . . multiplying and magnifying me and reminding me of my condition as a prisoner in this royal cell. I watch a dark line forming slowly on my lips, which little by little are losing their human appearance. Perhaps – why not? – I am also an animal, an armadillo feeding on insects and worms and beginning to feel, inside, the beginning of its final decomposition. Only beginning, Laura? For how long have your guts been rotting, the smell reaching under your tongue, between your teeth, in the sweat of your pores, which a gentle spray of Dior can no longer cover? The rouge hurts on the dull complexion. Blond lovers. Could it be that I chose them blond in reaction to Alberto? But I never hated him. . . . We both knew what we wanted from the other. We did play an underhand game, but always conscious of our fraud. Like civilized people never making remarks about our secret tricks. A civilized bed, hiding our embraces under the embroidered sheet, bodies struggling, with or without pleasure, always in the dark. The image of the Assumption of the Virgin that presides over the royal Falcon bed would never know, her demure eyes would never perceive that there below her hands joined in prayer and below her feet resting on a crescent moon a man and a woman procreated without a word, enduring without a whimper and drowning in unconfessed anger their private shame. If only we had talked sometimes, Alberto. . . . If we had dared to take off our animal-like masks. . . . Perhaps the warmth inside you, Laura, your sweet, welcoming, diamond skin. . . . Not to think of it. I moaned and cried on my wedding night. I played the role of the young bride to perfection, just as he had played that of a well brought up and correct fiancé. It was not difficult. It all had to come out right, without any mishap in this universe raised over infallible springs and whose brilliant structure aimed toward the joyful consummation of that great fossil: Ideal Happiness. The prediction of Doctor Bonecrasher, rapacious bird of the mountain, was fulfilled to the minute – one bleeds as if it were the first time. Although, of course it doesn't hurt. But he believed, or pretended to believe, that it hurt. If only that night when, already pregnant with Laurita, my body torn by permanent nausea, steaming with anger and disgust, I had approached him, daring to face him: "What do you think? I know perfectly well that it was not an accident that you have made me pregnant deliberately to hold me inside this house, this jail with golden bars, to care for your baby falcon, to knead docility as the slave kneads bread, to become a silent domestic animal, to annul myself ceaselessly chewing the same cud?" And all this after you promised me I would be free to live as I wanted. I even thought I could go back to the art school, reexperience the forgotten seduction of modeling with my hands, of the clay born from my hands, of the days when I fancied being a sculptor. Soft, malleable, in different colors, blended with laughter and dreams. Never. Yes, that day I should have dared to say, "Doctor Lynx, I am going to tell you a few secrets. For example, you must know that I was not a virgin when we married. I deceived you, of course. . . . Five years before we met, your special Laura, of the diamond skin, had fallen – oh! that terrible original sin! – fallen very much to her pleasure. I don't have to tell you with whom – his identity is secret – and what does it matter to you whom I went to bed with that first time anyway? What do you know of this, you old Lynx, accustomed to mount your wife like a docile mare, your sacred mare, of course. Mare-of-the-sun, Cow-of-the-sun? Nobody would dare to touch her, yet she is not untouchable, don't be deceived; the cow fucks behind your back, although she fulfils her duty with you because she is an animal of quality, good breed, and high price. She knows how to satisfy your needs, receiving you without protest into her noble cave for you to honor, fill, and perhaps impregnate, and immediately afterward fall asleep and snore all night, your head to the wall, sleep, snore. . . . The well-earned rest after the 'honest-day's-work of an honest worker.' Yet, if you want to know, if you are really interested, I will tell you. Yes, he was an art student like me ('Laura you are drunk'). Twenty years old and myself eighteen, just like in the words of the tango; he was delicate and pale and I fancied him to death ('Laura you must control your weakness for whisky, or we shall have to send you to a clinic for . . .')." Ernesto the Hippogryph, that was his name and that's what he was: half horse, half bird. The nerves and the strength for lovemaking, the impulse to reach the sky in a single flight of fantasy. Unreal. Monstrous. And by God, he had to fly away. . . . He wanted to be a sculptor, like me, and had created in his rented room a hellish setting of twisted irons, spirals that intertwined in upward motion, contorted silhouettes, epic masks that spied on us with faces destroyed by time. I was modeling shapes in clay and enamel. Animal shapes with human faces and humans with animal heads; an upside-down universe. It was not a gimmick; that's the way I saw the world, and he laughed at my imaginary inversions. Mother would howl in anger: "Some deal you are going to make going around with a starving man. Learn from your sister, you good-for-nothing; she is seriously engaged, soon to be married." Hilda was in love with that bank clerk; they had been meeting for three years hopping around on the blue sprung sofa, listening with well-contained anger to the muffled voice of grandfather narrating episodes of the civil war. Naturally, this admirer disappeared just when Hilda had started preparing her trousseau. The Great Mother, however, does not give up, but what can she hope for? Hilda is ugly, and one must lower one's expectations. With persuasive arguments, she personally approaches a certain Mr. Leadwaiter, manager of a store in the center of Union, a sober young man depending on his monthly salary. Hilda is still crying for her first loss when one evening Mother Skunk turns up as the Fairy Godmother triumphantly leading my present-day brother-in-law. Upright, half bald, yellow regular teeth, papier-mâché complexion, honest general appearance, he is formally introduced to the nubile young girl who, naturally ugly, still sports inflamed red eyes, crying for her loss. Mother serves chocolate and organizes one of our cheerful spontaneous little parties with anise cookies and father and grandfather relegated to the kitchen; father under strict maternal instructions to refrain the infantile, capricious curiosity of the old seal who insists on dragging his mischievous flat feet into the living room. I take advantage, in spite of Mother's anger – apparent behind the fire of her glances – with which she aims at melting, destroying, and annihilating me between one smile and another, I take advantage to slip away to Ernesto's. I live a moment of joy – how far away and long forgotten! Is this Laura stretched on a bunk, responding to the endless caresses of her body? I don't know on account of what . . . yes, now I know, but what is the point, it's too late. I don't know why we always quarreled after making love and he always talked of leaving; "But where?" I challenge him, "anywhere, Laura, where I may feel alive, away from this, to fight for human rights . . ." "Human rights," I tease him, "the fact is that you are afraid of staying here, Ernesto, to face what you have here, near you: poverty, for example. Besides, you are not sure of your art." In their motionless blindness the limbless, unfinished shapes sense our tension. "You are a coward, Ernesto." "Yes, but no more than you. Let's see, would you dare to leave your home and come with me?" I dare not tell him that I am afraid. Instead, I tell him that I despise him, that his remarks make me sick. That I will never come back. He slaps me. I run out into the street and run without stopping all the way home. From the corner I glimpse the rigid silhouette of my mother by the window. They are all asleep except her. She is rehearsing her great tragic scene in the same space where not long ago she has celebrated the first rite of Hilda's engagement: "Ungrateful daughter, who keeps rolling in bed with that starving man until he gives you an equally starving baby. But you will regret it, I swear," and she kisses her crossed fingers four times. I finally shout at her the true expression of my open rebellion, the only time when the armadillo lifts its muzzle and stands up in front of the world, my airless world of daily humiliations: "Shut up! What about your life?" She collapses on the blue armchair. I now know that she's no longer acting, that she is overcome by her own tears, not the ones prepared for me. The tears she regrets but can't hold back, to which I join my own, irreconcilable to her attitude but strangely bound. She is speaking rapidly. Her voice – I can remember it clearly because it was a different voice and she, my mother, unrecognizable: "Total unhappiness, my life – that's why I don't want the same for you. I made you pretty. I don't know how, because your poor father is a total disaster and I am ugly. But I desperately wanted to make you pretty – and I succeeded. I want you to be happy, very happy," she calls out. And I say to myself: "Happy, yes happy." And once again I run out into the street into the vertiginous deserted pavements that ambush me. I arrive at Ernesto's place, a dilapidated attic in an ancient building of the Old City. I hurry up the stairs, the rotting wood creaks under my feet. I stumble on a missing step, fall, get up again; I think I have squashed a cockroach with my finger, that I am seeing the metallic body of a rat disappearing round the corner like a flash. But I keep going through the thick darkness that envelops me from all sides. I reach his landing, the door is open. He always leaves the door open, but this once it is more open than ever. His room damp and gloomy receives me like a gigantic mouth. Trembling, I call him. No answer. I turn the light on and see the disaster: everything destroyed into pieces, pulverized, with an axe or a machete or perhaps even hit by frenetic blows. Our universe lies there contorted, agonizing as if an army of mad dwarfs had galloped over each one of the objects in that tumbledown room. I return to the street, no longer afraid though I know he has gone and that we shall never look for each other and never meet again. The Old City sleeps, withdrawn in its own silence. Unexpected, the prolonged wail of the siren from a boat is heard; it curls around the buildings, gets tangled in the tree branches to die eventually in the wind rising from the harbor. Nobody is in the street, but in the distance crackles the stentorian voice of a drunkard. I am alone in the world, naked after such a disaster. I must accept this solitude, which reminds me that I am still alive in the midst of the rubble and the ashes. I quicken my step; for the first time I feel the cold of dawn in my bones. At home I find her asleep in the armchair. A rhythmic rattle exits from her

mouth. I look at her and, though still in a mist, I begin to understand. Understand that perhaps it is better for him to have gone
and never come back. That what she had stated with such force
could be true: I must be happy – and I wasn't happy with Ernesto
– and I must procure myself another man, yes, "procure." It is im-
perative that I do, for my mother, for the "total disaster" of my
father, for my paralytic grandfather and my ugly sister and above
all for me, great actress that I am, whom are you trying to take in?
Even in the middle of the shipwreck, you thought that you won't
find happiness on a rickety bunk bed but in a golden bed, that
happiness is golden, all over, and that what she had just thrown in
your face was true, irrevocably so: you had chosen beauty not for
the sake of Ernesto the Hippogryph, molding clay and iron as well
as love with his hands, but for somebody else, somebody with a
different touch in his far-reaching safe hands; hands like claws
that build and destroy entire worlds because they are worlds
assembled by their resources, owned and dominated by them.
Hands . . . Yes I should have had the courage to say: "I'm going to
tear your embryo out of my belly, Alberto, tomorrow morning.
Not even God can save it." But I didn't and I now beat my belly as
I did then. What an idiot! Am I delirious? As if what I have now
were a new pregnancy. Laura Diamond Skin, female of a lynx,
what you have is – if I may put it this way – another form of pregnancy: you have fertilized yourself. So, understand and rejoice for
you have achieved freedom, the freedom of a hermaphrodite, but
in the end, freedom. Thanks to a repulsive, undrinkable dose of
bluish antimony. Congratulations! Feeling nauseous? Slightly so.
Together with spasms at the pit of the stomach. Have another
whiskey. Help yourself, the American bar is at your disposal. Laura
is helping Laura. It's all very relaxed and peaceful. Friends till
death. Three ice cubes, please. Thank you. Ice has a calming,
soporific effect. It will ease your discomfort. I used to suck ice
from the start of my pregnancies. Every half hour the maid

brought me a silver pot full of transparent ice cubes in which merged all the colors of the sky. At times I melted the ice in lemon juice and drank the cold acid potion in small comforting sips. I also tried to forget my nausea by reading. During my pregnancies I read all that I had neglected during my lazy adolescence. I discovered Dostoevsky, adored the Idiot Prince – we could have held and understood each other so tenderly and so generously, and died in a long, calm embrace. I also loved the characters of Balzac and Flaubert. In my sixth month, with my belly I took up poses of a Madame Bovary in front of the golden oval mirror that occupied my bedroom. I was deliciously embarrassed by the satanic ravings of Baudelaire. I imagined secret delights and projected them on his black mistress. I fed also on the classics: went wild with Antigone, died with Phaedra. Phaedra the brave, beyond all human measures, eternal . . . Another whiskey and this makes three. The ice has melted. Must make it to the fridge. One, two, "My dear lady you look a little, a little . . ." "Drunk!" Go ahead say it, Daniel, darling, my second blond lover, a kid and a violinist, single shoot and heir of Industrial Father and Matronly Mother. Sweet melodious Finch, made for music. The letter of introduction they gave you, young man. You don't have to thank me, no need for ceremonies between us. How did I fall into your musical arms? "Dear Doctor Lynx, I am sending you my son who has already distinguished himself in the musical college in our Paysandú. He is only seventeen and, as you can see, very timid. Since I only have business contacts in the capital – and remembering the confidence you have shown me as lifelong friend and client – I am asking you to be so kind as to help him along in his first steps: the boy wishes to complete his studies in the National College of Music. . . ." I went personally to meet him at Carrasco Airport. He got off the plane, his eyes were glazed, the eyes of a nervous inquisitive bird. Fragile and anxious, I recognized him by the timid fluttering of his wings. "Look Alberto, if you like, we can put him up. The guest room is empty. . . ." "But you just said that now with the baby you didn't want any more responsibilities." "H is a very quiet boy, and I would like to listen to his violin." He stayed. Locked up in his room, hermetic, unapproachable. He only appeared in front of us for his meals, through which he rushed without a word. Laurita was bellowing in her cot, and I'd tiptoe softly to his locked door. He played for hours on end, Schubert, Schumann, and Paganini at times. One day I knocked. Four loud knocks against the polished oak. It was seven in the evening, two hours to dinner time. He had been playing the same tune for three hours. He opens immediately and blushes at seeing me. "Come and have a whiskey with me, Daniel." He stutters something, becomes pale, and doesn't know how to behave. It's all so new and the assault has been so unexpected and so direct. What did you think, Daniel? My fourth whiskey for your thoughts. I'll tell you: "What is happening to this woman? I can't imagine that she . . . at least six or seven years older. And she is so formal and has a baby a few months old. But she is beautiful." And so you came to the terrace. Sat in front of me in the hammock, which started rocking you in time with your growing anxiety. "What were you playing?" "Grieg." "I have never heard it before." "It's a rather unknown study." His hand trembled reaching for the glass. He drank in one gulp. So did I. Like children playing: who drinks most and fastest. We had run out of ice. I got up and took two steps. "I am just going to the kitchen." My head was spinning – no, you pretended once more, liar! Pretended in order to have him take you by the arm to support you. Because you were afraid of your own daring. Because you wanted and didn't, you always hesitated after the first impulse. Coward. It's not true. I was drunk and told him so: "Drunk, yes, Daniel, my boy, I am drunk and not just a little. Completely." And fell on top of him and he received me in his arms and there in the hammock. A fury colored with songs. The world danced and Laurita in the bedroom on the same terrace was crying a million miles away. Yielding desperately to an uncontrollable anxious burning, like two enemies who drown in the same water and must hold on to each other. With anger and disgust, "Is this the timid child," I joked, "the gentle hands of the violinist. Beethoven, Bach, Chopin . . ." "What about you, Laura," he stammered, "You're not much better." And he wanted to start again. He had grown up suddenly and his eyes had clouded over. "I thought these things didn't matter to you. That's what your father said in his letter." And I moved away, laughing. He shouted: "You're drunk!" and I teased him: "Does mummy's boy want to be nursed?" "You're all the same, you society ladies! Dirty dipso, you disgust me," was his answer. I was also disgusted, but this was not new to me. Disgusted with his congested cheeks, with my sterile drunkenness, with his youthful violence, inconsistent like a summer storm. With his trembling fingers that shook the ice cubes in the glass. I wanted to antagonize him: "It was the first time, wasn't it?" "Whore!" he shouted. The pain starts. "And this will be the second." "Whore!" As if bad language would frighten me. I know it already, Daniel. I know all the officially called obscene words that appear in the dictionary and also those that are part of a more picturesque street jargon, censured, of course, in our respectable circles, although not ignored. I have a good memory and have always been intrigued by the richer veins of language. The pain increases. You had foreseen it all, Laura, nothing to worry about. "Sharp contractions at the base of your belly as when you need to go to the toilet," the doctor explained during one of the classes on "painless labor." "Push, my dear, push." A moan, a deep breath, a punch. To push my innards out, turn myself inside out, like a sock, to shoot that bundle into the intent face of the doctor who awaits with his pincers-like, urchin fingers carefully placed between my lifted legs, so ridiculous in their white leggings. "It's coming, another push. I can see the head." Still curious, faced with an everyday spectacle that is never the same. Eager and surprised: "It's going to be blond." What a joke, Alberto, an unexpected twist of fate. Underhanded mockery of your virile ambition. The son you longed for, blond and fragile with the delicate hands of a violinist. "To carry on the name." "Congratulations, my friend." He is back home already: "Fancy having a blond child . . . the caprices of nature." Without a word I concentrate on squeezing my breast to satisfy the insatiable hunger of the newborn. My nipples are covered in sores, bleeding painfully. I could not, would not feed him. I let him scream his head off at night. "You're being cruel, Laura, you weren't like this with Laurita." All I wanted was to sleep and sleep. I had fallen into a golden state of lethargy, which nobody had the right to disturb. Alberto tried to counsel me: "You shouldn't drink. You're weak. Shouldn't give into vice." And he stressed the word *vice*. He was always impressed by the emptiness of the abstract terms that he used to adorn the entourage of his idols and fans. "Honor, justice, geniality": the three beautiful virtues with which he invested the great tyrannosaur of his father. "Modesty, simplicity, goodness" were the epitomes of quality that befell his fishlike mother. I don't know with what abstractions he endowed me. He liked me, I don't doubt it, in his way, but he never looked for me. He never dared to really look at me. What has our living together, our misery, our love, got to do with love. Love is just one more word, sterile, incongruent, wasted with usage that we never understood. It was left there over my dressing table like an empty jar. Useless both, false, remote. Armadillo and a Falcon-Lynx. . . . Impossible crossing.

Mother would come to the house everyday. She too preached about my vice and ended up by crying, sorrowfully stretching out in my direction the hand of a gloved weasel. She opened and shut the silver clasp of her handbag, avid like the mouth of the baby crying out in the evenings: "I can understand being unfaithful, if you know how to do it discreetly. But to burden him with somebody else's child . . ." I laughed and she left in anger because she understood that her unselfish maternal reproaches did not worry me any more. Or perhaps she might have suddenly remembered that her younger daughter had a good memory. I was always praised for it in school, and how she liked to hear the teacher say I was "the-best-of-the-class." Good memory, mother, to remember well your scandalous escapades. "Poor mummy has a toothache." Sometimes she took me along. Hilda stayed at home to finish up the jobs our moaning mother had to abandon. The dentist embraced her and she: "Please, doctor, please," increasing her pitch with her facility for easy rhyming. And then tragically: "The child!" Blindly, I concentrated on looking at the glass case with its steel instruments: varied, incomprehensible forms whose twisted joints seemed to gesture at me in complicity. Afterward running along the streets because it was getting late: "Your poor mummy must come all alone tomorrow to have a tooth out" – pretty mummy, whore of a mummy. It never happened to Hilda. Who on earth would make for her? Thirty-five years and now a block of melting fat. Leggy, ungainly bird, turned, after laborious metamorphosis, into a gigantic sow. With four children, a ton each. One of them – the second or the third ton – the godchild of Doctor Lynx, and mine, of course.

The contractions are getting stronger. As painful as during the first labor. More whiskey. The only remedy. It always was the only remedy. And think of something else. The third lover. A very beautiful object: elastic muscles, iron biceps, Apollonian posture. Naïvely, I thought that within the challenge of such well-rounded, strong flesh there could be a somebody – not just an object – disguised, hidden by this dazzling appearance. Golden mornings on the beach of Punta del Este. By the water, the improvised colony of aquatic mums senselessly intent on chatting away: "You're quite slim again, Laura." "You get your figure back so easily." "I'm always on a diet and don't lose an ounce." The sun envelops me in ecstatic torpor. Their trivial, garrulous conversation reaches me, but I don't see them. They are my friends who mean nothing to me. I allow myself to drown in sunshine. Possessed by it, not a violent but a soothing, pleasurable possession. The very goal of an organism voluptuously stretched to the tips of my nails and of all my hairs. A more seductive embrace, sweeter than that of most men. Sweeter and paradoxically more human. Elia whispers: "There he goes," and Julieta: "What a hunk." Irma discreetly touches me: "Look at him, Laura, the German we talked about. He teaches children to swim." I have no desire to sit up, nor to open my eyes. "You mustn't miss him, he is a real treat." I insist in not getting up. Suddenly Irma warns: "He's coming our way," and Elia: "He's coming to our sun-shade: pass me a mirror and a comb." I sit up, drowsy, drunk with sun. On the seashore I see a pile of shellfish moving slowly, sliding on their abdomens: crayfish, spotted carp, small blue crabs. The image fades, gives in to that of the man. More than human, heroic in its lightening splendor. Not German, son of Germans. Speaks perfect Spanish and five more languages. Shines like a Greek god. A Tiger, but tamed. He kindly offers to teach our children how to swim: "Mine are still little," I protest. He looks at my half-open legs while he explains that it is better to start them very young. He looks at my shoulders, the cleavage that rises over the cut of my bathing costume. My friends cluck maliciously, and Julieta, feeling left out, enigmatically suggests: "Would you like to sit a while with us? . . ." He sits. We talk of Europe: "Have you traveled much?" "Yes indeed, I have even lived in the Far East. . . ." He likes mountain climbing, skiing, is a tennis champion. The prototype of an Olympic athlete. I invite him to a party in my chalet at San Rafael. He comes. His skin dazzles and is warm; dancing with him I feel the heat of the sun. I notice that Alberto looks at him with admiration and envy. One evening we go swimming at an isolated beach. The sea roars, waves rise like castles and collapse in a fury at our feet. Can't swim. But I didn't go there to swim. I went to sleep with him, admit it Laura. I come out of the water shivering with cold. He covers me with a white towel and together we lie by a dry bush. . . . I feel sick. Must go to the toilet. You don't have to go that far. You can vomit over the Persian carpet. Nobody is coming today or tomorrow. No need to tidy up the old shack. The family is enjoying itself in Punta del Este, while this house acquires its natural appearance of a pigsty. The whole family less you, Laura. Even my mother. Incredible, but Alberto agreed to it this weekend. To hell with him, they understand each other: the Skunk and the Lynx, both carnivorous mammals with foulsmelling mouths. They more than understand each other for their dubious, unconfessed intrigues. Happy weekend: whiskey on the terrace, the smell of pine in the air, purity to renew the spirit. And the visit of the Primal-Dogheads or of the Rattlesnakes and Weasels, and of the Sons-of-Bitches. All God's creatures. God's own fauna. Uncovering their ulcers in the open to scratch each other in a friendly gesture of real philanthropy. Yet you, too, have lived, up to last week, in the tepid warmth of their putrefaction. You are not going to take a heroic stand now, are you? I am not heroic, I am just revolted. . . .

"This nausea, doctor, I can't get rid of it. . . . And I can't bear this insomnia any more." "Perhaps your nervous system is worn out. I'll start by prescribing a tonic for your nerves. You lead a rather hectic life." Obviously he wanted to know about me, not as a doctor but as a man facing an attractive woman. "Actually, doctor . . ." I was puzzled. And he . . . Alexis – a redhead rather than blond. With freckles elegantly distributed on his nose and cheeks. And green eyes, deep eyes, calm as the water of a pond. A dolphin, the most intelligent of all sea creatures, an acrobat, responsive to training, quick to jump. Disguising his sharp understanding behind a sympathetic professional interest in human nature. I went to see him because life had become too much. You are lying, Laura. You were looking for a new adventure, craving for an escape. And met, unexpectedly, with a dangerous trained Dolphin.

One had to dive deep to deal with him. I really did fall in love. My face there in the mirror: deep bags under my eyes, a light mauvish shade on the cheek bones. The same story goes on unpredictably. Nothing new, you know. Events weave on with precise accuracy. But not that day, when the unknown was unknown. I remember the fear, real horrible fear. Yet it was not the first time that a hostile body stirred between my legs, turned over my sex. But it was the first abortion. That face never to be seen again, half covered by the stretched mask. The wise old white-haired nurse, a fat quail with a sorrowful expression, stroking my arm. Legs wide while a pointed spoon, the kind used to serve exotic sauces, scraped my insides. But I was asleep. . . . Total anesthesia, of course. Sleep is a great resource, an escape. On my left, when I rise from my lethargy, I catch sight of that brutal picture: kind physician snatching the exhausted woman from the arms of the skeleton of death; medicine at the service of the good and health overcoming Evil and Death. I opened my legs with shame, for life to be snatched out of me. No, not with shame. With fear. Bloodcurdling fear. Yet I skillfully played the part, when sorrowfully I heard the voice of the nurse saying: "The doctor says that it is better to get rid of it, because you are very weak and a pregnancy could . . ." Thank you, dear white-haired madam. . . . Laura did not want any more pregnancies, nausea, sickness, children. And she paid for this with the touch of the cruel anonymous hand turning her guts out, the cold sweat that dampened her diamond skin, and the localized unexpected pain once the anesthetic wore off. Warm new blood flowed out of her sex as if life sadly, pitifully, left with it. It would have been Alexis's child. Nevertheless, you mustn't lie: you weren't in love with him. Your third child from your fourth love, drowned in an aseptic bowl. Others had tested my sexual inadequacy, and I was desperate. Couldn't bear it any longer. I hung on to him as a last resort. . . .

Golden colors on the façades of buildings. I've made it as far as

the window and from here . . . I've already vomited twice. This
is the third. On the handsome green carpet, "like a meadow in
your house," as the decorator described it. The floor of the pigsty.
There, another large whiskey. With lots of ice. Sick again, and the
pain and the nausea . . .

The tenth floor. His skyscraper apartment from which you
tower over the city. His hands running up and down my body . . .
Alexis. "How can you possibly not feel anything? You are built for
pleasure. A voluptuous shape covered in fine sensitive down . . ."
Soft the palms of his hands, soft his voice and protective, its reas-
suring tone. For once it was all happening without any violence:
"There must have been something in your past, Laura, in your
childhood: we will find it. Perhaps your parents . . ." And you told
him everything. Fell in the trap of the trained dolphin, cold mind,
warm blood. You told him how, during the Saturday siesta, you,
pretending to sleep curled up in your bed, saw his insignificant
figure coming up the stairs, heard the wild screams of that whore
of your mother, satisfying her vaginal hunger. And the man's
insults, always humiliated, growing from the blind circle of his
obscenities, once a week to be devoured by that enormous spider
in her cave. Then the gasps and your painful amazement. And pre-
cociously a feverish desire awakened inside you. "It was not preco-
cious, Laura, children's sexuality emerges very early." Wordless
wanderings in the world of images, in the monstrous darkness of
your childhood insomnia. The weave is ripping apart . . . it hurts
. . . Alexis is on top of me. And not so soft. The acrobatic dolphin
suddenly becomes a gigantic hippocamp riding on my disarmed
body. Horse of the sea indeed, violent and hard like bone, powerfully erected and falling down on top of me, a lightning scourge.
He meant to discover you – so he said – cancel your complexes,
bring back to life your sense of pleasure, your passion . . . Afterward, aloof and without a word, he stretched out by your side
and escaped into the currents of his bottomless sea. I dressed my

shameful body, which now felt abused ever since my freshly redis-covered childhood. Love, trust, abandon. "Nothing but words," I shouted, riding alone in the lift. I never saw him again – last memory of him, the inconsolable abortion. The rest: a blind woman hitting in the dark, senseless kicking of the armadillo sud-denly granted by some perverse power, unsolicited partial con-sciousness. Embrace a cause? Go back to art, work, earn my living, study? The universe sinks into colorless, shapeless slime. A vast flat surface stretching out yet so near and so pitifully destructive. The final resolution: to wean myself throughout, in one go.

The city is lit up, Laura. Day is over. Nearby the neon signs flash in the avenue. Blue and purple blushes color the faces of build-ings and fade into a strange golden mist. I can hardly see or feel. My eyes . . . everything is totally, uniformly golden. The diamond necklace around my neck is tightening. My fingers can't feel it, yet . . . they have now dropped the glass of whisky. . . .

Translated from the Spanish by Psiche Hughes

In Florence Ten Years Later

It was the same main square with its Duomo, Santa Maria del Fiore, the smooth white and dark marble stripes constantly beckoning, inviting you to steep yourself in its intimate structure. Florence, rounded arches and columns stretching out along the valley towards Peretola, Sesto Fiorentino, and the sea. The city famous for the most beautiful dresses and shoes, fabulous jewels, and ceramics; the place where she thought she would find that longed-for happiness. So much had changed within her since then. . . . Nowadays she wouldn't dream of wasting time to even glance at Doctor Schnabl's books: she has lost her patience – and her confidence.

She was walking on the pavement of Palazzo Strozzi, having ignored the eastern door of the Baptistery, which depicted scenes from the Old Testament, its prophets and sibyls, and the northern one, which represented evangelists and scholars of the early Latin church. She did not know which of the two Michelangelo had judged worthy of being the gate to paradise and regretted not having Jacques's learned comments, his archaeological competence. A long time had passed since that night when, after a bottle of rosé, they had made love in a cheap pensione by the Arno. Her mind fixed on the Apollonian trunk of the *David* seen a few hours before in the Accademia: the narrow hips and muscled calves of a dancer, not at all like Donatello's pensive shepherd. A famished and effeminate figure in bronze, resting the immovable weight of his sword on the ground.

She had come back to Florence, oblivious of everything but Michelangelo's impetuous *David*, whose copy in front of the

Palazzo della Signoria was now seducing her. She identified with Bathsheba, beloved of the heroic king who, in the throes of overwhelming desire, had sent her husband, Urias, to sure death in the battlefield. This was the real David, drawn out of the imposing block of marble by Buonarroti's will, that very block that Agostino d'Antonio and even Leonardo da Vinci had not dared to tackle, and which Florentines, equally sharp in wit as in battle, had nicknamed "The Giant."

Nobody had ever reminded her so much of Bebo as that unique sculpture, its projecting scrotum that, knitted with curly tufts of pubic hair, makes the penis appear smaller and easier to handle. How different from the superb dimensions of Jacques's member, rigid yet vulnerable between the sacks of the hanging testicles. At some stage she had even thought that it was Jacques's penis that most corresponded to that of the *David*, with its marble firmness and protruding veins at the climax of an erection. Now, though, looking at it carefully, David's penis had the correct proportions, given that he was about to confront the giant Goliath and hurl the stone out of his sling.

That night in the pensione she had hardly the time to fantasize about clutching the narrow pelvis of the statue (Bebo's elusive, agile, and playful hips) because, as usual, only a few seconds after entering her, Jacques had reached his climax. There was no point in suggesting that he take up a certain therapy advised by Doctor Schnabl for this kind of problem, even less in asking him to go on caressing her clitoris with his tongue or his fingers. Her lack of assertiveness in these matters was not entirely due to false modesty, the result of her prudish and old-fashioned education. She had grown accustomed to being excited by the man's excitement. It would be more disappointing to have her contented husband carry on for her sake than to end their lovemaking as they always did: with Jacques holding her tight against him for some time, as if to make up for the brevity of their encounters. He would caress her hair tenderly, manifesting his gratitude in poetic whispers. Yet he never thought of asking if she were satisfied and showed no sign of having enough energy to repeat his performance. Out of delicacy or shyness, she remained silent, often telling herself that with a little patience she might learn to achieve her pleasure more quickly. Yes, it was all a matter of patience and of not losing confidence.

Without a doubt, Michelangelo's *David* was the spitting image of Bebo, with his mixture of pride and defiance, ready to leap into unlimited space. Something in the statue's expression recalled the look of her ex-lover that day on the promenade of Havana, when she announced she was going to marry Jacques and go with him to Italy after a few days in Paris in the Hôtel Messidor in the rue Vaugirard. Bebo had stared at her with the disdain of a beggar who knows he owns the world, being able to adjust to any situation, and then suggested a friendly farewell in a room in Calle San Lázaro. They used to meet there regularly until that fateful night a few months before when, without any explanation, he'd gone off alone to the dance in the gardens of the Club Tropical, in spite of their previous arrangement. That same fateful night when she met Jacques.

Bebo asked her to strip for him and even joked about how slim she had become. The healthy diet proposed by Jacques, who was determined to turn her into an "honorary" European, had visibly reduced the layer of fat that timidly surrounded her belly. But her solid hips and high buttocks remained the same under the silk flared skirt that Bebo had ignored. He moved rapidly toward her muttering sweet obscenities: words that stimulated those glands unknown to Jacques and produced a miraculously rich lubrication. Such uncontrollable secretions were never to dampen the sheets of hotels and pensiones scattered along the tortuous routes from Paris to Padua, to Venice, to Urbino, and, through Florence, to Naples.

The question of language never figured in the bibliographies that she obsessively began consulting: books by sexologists like Masters and Johnson and Siegfried Schnabl, especially the chapters about frigidity and inability to reach orgasm, and the one that could have been written just for her and Jacques, entitled "Is the Sex Act Too Brief?" Pity that she never found anything about the stimulating power of words. She had never imagined needing verbal communication to reach an orgasm, and was slightly alarmed when she read an article in a scientific magazine by a Danish doctor about a pathological condition called *coprolalia* – the morbid inclination to voice dirty words. Perhaps Bebo suffered from this rare aberration. Though she went on searching, she never discovered whether this condition also applied to those who, like her, enjoyed listening to rather than saying the words. What would David have whispered to Bathsheba in Urias's absence during those long nights when Solomon was conceived? "What a gorgeous cunt you have," or "Amore mio, ti voglio tanto bene"?

She knew that vulgar terms to describe the reproductive organs and the sexual act existed in all languages, but in French, Jacques's language, those nouns sounded so innocuous, even slightly musical. She found nothing exciting in her husband's using the word *baiser*, which ultimately meant nothing but to kiss, or calling the vagina *la chatte* and the penis *la queue*. It seemed like a child's game, to strip lovemaking of its transgressive connotations and turn it into an innocent masquerade of zoological metaphors.

Now walking toward the Accademia, by the convent of San Marco, with its smooth walls and small windows, she remembered a Chilean, great admirer of Beato Angelico, whom she had met in Toulouse in 1995 when, in her loneliness during one of Jacques's business trips, she was touring the provinces. By then she had lost both patience and confidence. By then Clarita, her godmother in Havana, had decided that Jacques would never be the man to give her the pleasure so famously described by Schnabl – "But he gives you everything else. Don't risk changing what you have for what might never be."

Clarita, however, tolerated reports of the sporadic presence of some other man – as long as he was not Bebo – met on the way, just to have some fun. Gonzalo – forty-three years old, with the briefcase of a multinational executive, chivalrous manners, and responsible behavior – appeared on the scene and promised fulfillment between those sterile, fleeting encounters with Jacques – now less and less frequent – that took place under the eiderdown, on a bed over which hung a copy of the *Last Supper* in the house of his mother, Adele, where she languished with boredom and nostalgia.

Inventing all kinds of lies to offset the suspicions of this nosy woman who rigorously watched her every movement, she managed a clandestine trip to exciting Amsterdam with Gonzalo. There they visited the Van Gogh Museum and afterward made love in the apartment of some of his Chilean compatriots, addicted to the songs of the group Cedrón. Though alarmed that her fantasies about the *David* or her hallucinations about Bebo's vocabulary might recur, she grew contented in the arms of that experienced lover. He knew how to control his excitement and wait for her, how to induce her pleasure by slow and relaxed foreplay, endowed with subtle caresses and delicate tricks.

All this, however, lacked the fun and gay vitality she had known with Bebo. Though they spoke the same language, Gonzalo did not have the gift of expressing his sensuality in words. He remained silent and serious as one who carries out a delicate task, beautifully, attentive of his partner's reactions, but invariably distant. Like Jacques, he held her close to him after making love. Still naked, they would drink rosé and talk. They spoke mainly of Florence, the Ponte Vecchio, and Angelico's frescoes, in which he had for the first time discovered realism (that of the fifteenth century). He talked of the way Angelico inserts himself in the world of saints and giants and gives them nobility and class. That same nobility with which he refused Pope Eugenio IV's offer of becoming the city's archbishop, in order to carry on caring for the sick and painting.

Gonzalo also liked the *David*, but he preferred the *Moses* that adorns Pope Giulio II's tomb in Rome, a product of the artist's maturity. From Gonzalo she learned that Michelangelo suffered from panic attacks. He believed he benefited from foresight: he did not mold the marble gradually but entered the stone and dragged out the form in layers, shaping the forehead first so that the lower limbs appeared as if born in the very block. At times he hurled away his hammer and chisel, saying to himself, "If I stay here one more minute, something terrible will happen to me." He then would buy a horse and ride to Bologna or Rome. The first time this occurred was in 1492 after the death of Lorenzo de Medici, the patron who taught him to favor Plato, Saint Augustine, and Saint Paul. The *David*, created around 1501, is witness to the tortured, dissatisfied sensibility that Spengler described as "the terrible" of Michelangelo's shapes.

The meetings with Gonzalo held the fascination of the forbidden (he was married to a Belgian violinist who was often away on tours across the continent), and those escapades had to some extent replaced the transgressive quality that Bebo's language gave to their lovemaking. Yet there was something strained in the behavior of the Chilean – perhaps his effort to feel integrated in a culture to which neither of them belonged. What she liked was his smell, the slight curve of his shoulders, of one who knows how to submit to the requests of his superiors, and his way of pronouncing his name, giving it a French intonation. This apart, Gonzalo never awakened in her that wet lust, the feverish shudders and repeated orgasms her body knew with her ex – ungrateful – lover. He who was right now finishing his prison sentence in Havana for stealing cotton balls for injections from the hospital where he worked.

She was thinking of all this on her way to the Accademia gallery, passing by Santissima Annunziata, listening to the discussions and the incisive judgments of the Florentines, when she made out the imposing shape of the marble statue at the end of the corridor. "To free the shape already contained in the stone, stripping it of the superfluous, of the dregs that imprison it in the raw material." This is what Michelangelo aimed to do before losing his patience and allowing those "dregs" to emerge, before he turned to the mannerism of his *Pietà*. When his sensuality was still directed by a feeling for the eternal, the remote, and not by the eroticism of the fleeting moment. The *David* suddenly in front of her was there to prove it – the powerful neck, the curly head, the large, experienced hands that knew how to caress Bathsheba. Was this also Bebo, just out of jail, the same one who, ten years earlier, refused to go with her to the dance at the Club Tropical? Bebo who had never ceased to whisper in her ears, with a half-broken voice, those coarse expressions of love and his irrevocable decisions? The same Bebo of their last meeting a few months ago in the always-present promenade of Havana when, desperate and sure that he was "the only man for her," she spoke to him of divorce, of her decision to forget Clarita's advice and leave Jacques; of having him near her forever, removing him from that hell of poverty and showing him Piazza San Firenze, Botticelli's *Primavera*, teaching him to drink rosé and speak Italian. Bebo, disguised as David, face turned to the side, resting the catapult on his shoulder, his body ready to fight to death the enemy of his people. Bebo, humming a song about an unfaithful woman and the cruel pain she caused him. Bebo, refusing to take her for the last time to the little room in Calle San

Lázaro, now propped up by scaffolding and with window frames chewed up by termites. Bebo, prepared to go on being interrogated by the police constantly prowling around the gate of the Club Tropical's garden. Bebo, believing in the elemental truths of a fashionable salsa –"You went and are lost, I stayed and am now king" – with absolute, incomprehensible, almost manic determination.

Translated from the Spanish by Psiche Hughes

Love Story

Teleca could simply not stay in bed.

I'm sure she's chatting away at the door. She leaned out of the balcony. The emptiness in the street hit her. She's locked herself in the bathroom. She does it to provoke me.

"Lupe! Lupe! Lupeee!" Teleca shouted in anger.

She could not think of anything else. Her relationship with Lupe had become an obsession. Just then she heard the tapping of her old shoes in the kitchen. "Where were you, Lupe?"

"Upstairs, ma'am."

"And what could you be doing there at this hour of the day?"

"Taking a shower."

Her black hair, all wet and tangled, was dripping over her shoulders, her waist, her back, and her buttocks; such long hair, held back with a red comb; a bundle of hair, heavy, like a horse's mane.

"You did tell me to wash myself often."

"But not during working hours."

As Lupe, still wet, confronted her, Teleca could see the red tree of resentment in her eyes.

"Bring me my breakfast."

"Okay."

"That's not the way to answer. Say, 'Yes, ma'am.'"

"Uh-huh."

"Say, 'Yes, ma'am,'" Teleca almost shouted.

The woman remained silent, then decided to comply. "Yes, ma'am."

Teleca walked out of the kitchen, slamming the door. Back in her bedroom she felt the need to walk around. She picked up one object after another, changed them around, mislaid them, went to and from the door like a lion in a cage. She was dying to go back to the kitchen to see what Lupe was doing now, look at her face, like a stone polished by water. To start afresh, find more suitable words: I'll wait another few minutes. She went to the bathroom and angrily brushed her hair. Thank God the phone rang. After a short delay, Lupe shuffled to answer it, then came back slowly and knocked on the door.

"It's for you."

Teleca's heart jumped. "You must say, 'There's a telephone call for you, ma'am.' Besides, you took ages to pick it up."

No this was not the right tone, she wanted to sound relaxed; a smile began to quiver over her lips, and there it was on the point of opening up. Lupe's mane of hair was still dripping. Teleca moved her aside.

"Hello? Arturito? Hi, good to hear from you. How are you? Me? Oh, so so. A bit agitated. Don't know why, domestic problems, maybe. These people just don't understand. There is no way to get close to them. At least, I can't. Yes, of course I know there are other topics of conversation, but this is what is happening right now and I need to talk about it. If only to get some relief. At Lady Baltimore's? At five o'clock? Sure, great! Thank you. Goodbye."

Teleca walked toward the kitchen. How can a miserable Indian reduce me to this state? How can it be? It's not right. It's because I'm so lonely. . . .

"Lupe, my breakfast."

"Yes, ma'am."

At least she had said, Yes, ma'am.

Lupe brought the tea, a soft-boiled egg, and toast. The cup shone white, as did the cubes in the equally white sugar bowl. Teleca had already drunk her orange juice.

"Did the newspaper come?"

"I'll see."

"Haven't I told you the first thing to bring me in the morning is the paper? And lay it on the table by my side. I bet it's wet by now."

The maid returned with *El Universal*, her face an expressionless mask.

"Lupe, the marmalade, why haven't you put the marmalade on the table? And the butter?"

"You told me not to, a month ago. You didn't want to put on weight."

"I am no longer on a diet."

"Okay."

"You don't say 'Okay'! How many times must I tell you to answer, 'Yes, ma'am'?"

Teleca tried to concentrate on the headlines but realized they did not matter to her. All that mattered was Lupe, to know what she thought, to follow her, stand by her in front of the sink, look at her arms, round and solid, her arms, apple trees in leaf – she liked the way the skin of her fingers wrinkled in the water. To hear her young voice flow like the water on her hands. Secretly, Lupe must be aware of the power she had over her mistress; she was frowning, and her proud mouth had formed a nasty grimace.

After breakfast, Teleca went to the kitchen. "I'm going to take a bath."

Lupe remained silent.

"Listen for the telephone and the door."

"Uh-huh."

Teleca's nerves were once more on edge. She could easily have raised her hand against the woman, pulled that bundle of wet hair that weighed on her Indian, Indian, Indian shoulders. But she would also have liked to see her smile, eyes shining, cheeks beaming – amazing how dark skin shines after being washed. And hear her singsong voice, as it was at first, say, "Is everything all right, ma'am?" Everything's all right, all right, all right.

But nothing was right. Teleca went about her daily washing routine all taken with the thought of Lupe. She tried to anticipate her expression at one o'clock: a friendly gesture, sparkle in her eyes. She might be more agreeable by then.

She imagined the scene:

"I'm off, Lupe. Remember that I won't eat at home today. As I told you last night, I'm going to lunch with the Güemeses."

"Yes, ma'am. In that case I shall clean the silver. Have a good time, ma'am."

Sometimes Lupe had said, "Have fun," and Teleca still remembered it with gratitude. Of all her maids, Lupe had lasted longest. Living alone as she did, the person with whom she shared her house and so many hours was important to Teleca. At first she used the familiar form *tú* but, when she was annoyed, she marked their respective positions with a display of formality.

As I leave, I'll tell her casually to take the radio into the kitchen to keep her company, Teleca thought. But what is happening to me? I'm paying too much attention to Lupe as if she were all I had in my life. My nerves must be in a bad state. What will Lupe think of me? Does she care for me? Such a tight-lipped woman! Like a lump of dough without eyes.

At the door, Teleca put on her hat and, trying to sound cheerful, said, "Lupe, I'm going. See you at five."

Only the humming of the traffic from the Avenida Insurgentes answered her.

In a less amiable tone, Teleca shouted, "Lupe, I'm going! Have tea ready at five and don't scratch the silver! Please remember to use the right product and a soft cloth, not the dishcloth. No water and soap like you did last time!"

Her instructions were amplified by the ensuing silence.

"Lupe? Did you hear me?"

"Okay."

A funereal echo accompanied these words, which came from the kitchen, or the ironing room, or even the inside of a cupboard, or whatever airless dark recess that imbecilic smelly Indian woman inhabited. I don't know why I bother with such an animal. And Teleca stepped out with a purposeful stride. It will do me good to be with people of my own kind and to stop worrying about improving the lot of some helpless being. She walked toward the Güemeses's, her skirt fluttering around her legs, but at the first turn she stopped and was about to turn back. I forgot to tell her to take the radio into the kitchen. Then she remembered the "Okay," which had sounded slow, heavy like sludge. It will do her good, she thought, still wanting to educate the woman. She will miss me. I am sure she will miss me. An empty house is something horrible.

She glimpsed her own image years ago, alone in the kitchen, with nobody around to teach good manners; making tea, waiting for the whistle of the boiling kettle, listening for the bell, ready to start conversation with whoever came to the door – a salesman, the newspaper boy. Just like any street slut. She remembered the notes she had written to herself in her sharp handwriting learned at the convent of the Sacred Heart and hung in evidence in the kitchen or the corridor, not to remind herself, but for company. "Please keep door shut," "Turn the gas off," "Don't forget the keys before leaving," "The electricity bill is paid on the first Friday of the month," "Where there's a will there's a way." And, in big figures, the numbers that connected her with the outside world. Reliving that anguish, Teleca was about to scream, Help, I'm suffocating, or to run as she did to the Güemeses's house. She went in breathless, nervous, scared like a sparrow seeking refuge in the roof. "How are you? What a picture you make sitting together like that!" The Güemeses looked surprised at the sight of their friend all in a flutter. A picture, indeed, she thought. All they needed was a broom each. Teleca asked for the telephone: "I forgot to leave instructions for Lupe."

"Teleca, be quick. We are starting with a soufflé."

"Delicious – I'm so hungry. I won't be a minute."

She picked up the receiver. Heard the tone spreading in the air, a signal without answer. Why was that lazy Indian taking so long?

She dialed again. The third time came an answer: "Lupe?"

"Uh-huh."

"Haven't I told you? . . . Look, you must also clean my father's Polo Cup. You haven't done it for a long time and it's pretty dirty."

"What?"

"The Polo Cup."

"What cup?"

"Can't you hear me? The cup he won for playing polo, the tall silver one with handles shaped like a swan. I forgot to tell you."

"You mean the biggest cup in the room?"

"Yes, that one, Lupe." She was about to say "my dear," but controlled herself.

"I don't know whether I'll have product enough . . ."

"Why didn't you buy more?"

"You haven't left me any money."

She would have liked to carry on chatting with Lupe, but the Güemeses were calling her: "Teleca, Teleca." It had been so pleasant to talk to Lupe on the telephone, which seemed to be molding in her hand, without seeing her sullen, stony, impenetrable face. Teleca was in the habit of calling home to give instructions, verifying that Lupe was there. She would call over and over until she got an answer and then reproach her: "Where were you? Who gave you leave to go out? You are not a child, and you know you must not leave the house empty. That's why you all (and she had in mind a long procession of housemaids, a constellation of women with aprons and hair in plaits, coming toward her in her desert), that's why you are all in that condition, because you are irresponsible, unfit, stupid, you have no ambition, no self-respect, no desire to come out of your lethargy." She thought of Lupe's face – not a single muscle moving.

"And if Señor Arturito calls, tell him I'm having lunch at the Güemeses's."

"But you spoke to him this morning."

"I forgot to tell him."

"Ah, yes." Lupe spoke without conviction.

"Did you open the bathroom window? You must hang the towels in the sun before the rain comes. You always forget."

Teleca was angry with the Güemeses for interrupting her conversation but had to give in. "I'll call later to see what's happened." She heard a mutter that very much sounded like one of Lupe's "uh-huhs" and the click of the receiver. Wretched, miserable woman, she put the receiver down before I did. Didn't even give me the time to say goodbye. I'm going to make her pay for it. I'll call her after coffee.

People with obsessions have the rare power of drawing everybody else to the center of their spiral, tightening its grip, closing its circles at every turn until it reaches the breaking point. At the table, Teleca managed to turn the conversation to the topic of domestics, in French, of course, not to be understood by good old Josephine.

"How can it be that servants are so stupid?"

"If they weren't, they wouldn't be servants."

"These people are like animals. In France, England, and Spain, domestics are different. They know how to treat people according to whom they are talking, they are responsible. A different category. But these animals, who don't have two cents to rub together, aren't even grateful for what we do for them."

"Perhaps it's the sun: they're suffering from too much exposure to the sun."

"Or the Conquest."

"Yes, the Conquest. They lost everything then, even their sense of shame."

"It's a case of race. They lack gray matter."

Teleca went on speaking until coffee was served. It was her way of being near Lupe – to summon her presence, move around her. Plump and affable, one of the Güemeses tried to put an end to this outpouring.

"Why don't we play a game of bridge? We can take our cups to the coffee table."

They all agreed. At five o'clock Teleca screamed, "I've got an appointment with Arturito at Lady Baltimore's. How terrible! I'll never make it on time. I really should not have arranged it for today, knowing I was having lunch with you."

What actually annoyed her was not being able to call Lupe. How could she do it now, where and when? There was no way she could leave Arturito alone in the tearoom.

"Unfortunately our chauffeur is away, Teleca. He could have driven you."

"It doesn't matter, I adore taxi drivers."

Sipping his tea, Arturito, inspired by Teleca's comments, gave a long dissertation on the Conquest and its description by Bernard Díaz del Castillo. This was not what she needed. Nobody except Lupe gave her what she needed. If only Arturito would shut up, she could go. But Arturito, mad about history, was threatening a discussion on racial segregation in the States. Teleca's tummy began to hurt. Arturito stretched his arm toward her necklace.

"Do you know this amber hanging from your chain is worth ten slaves?"

"Because of the worm inside?"

"With the worm it's probably worth fifteen slaves."

"Let's go, Arturito."

And without further ado, without waiting for him, Teleca got up. There was something boyish in her rapidity that both disconcerted and attracted Arturito; her way of climbing the stairs, two by two, with those long, slim legs that seemed to gallop rather than walk. She had practically no hips and fixed her tea-colored eyes on you. Didn't they teach her when she was a little girl that this is not the way to look at people? And she smiled so openly from ear to ear, revealing large, strong, white teeth like grains of maize exposed to the sun and the wind. She also winked. "I can't help it," she said, whenever people commented on it.

"Teleca, I have arranged to play bridge at Lucerna. Can I drop you in my taxi on the way?"

"Thank you, Arturito. Are you playing with Novo and Villaur-rutía? Who's going to be the fourth?"

"Torres Bodet. Have you finished reading *Les Faux Monnay-eurs*?"

"I told you, my nerves are on edge and I can't concentrate."

"If you read, you would forget your nerves. Look" – Arturito leaned out of the window – "Look, it's almost dark. In Mexico, night falls suddenly. Either nothing happens and a layer of boredom suffocates us, or some cataclysm occurs and disaster follows. What a country!"

"It's your country . . ."

Arturito smiled mockingly. "You're a bundle of contradictions, Teleca. Patriotism does not suit you. After all, you're always talking of moving to Spain."

"But in the meantime I defend darkness."

"The black holes of darkness?"

Teleca didn't answer. She felt a sharp sense of solidarity with Lupe. She was capable of kicking her, but in front of the rest of the world she passionately defended anything Indian: the land, the woods, the maize, the beans, and the heated rocks.

"Look, it hasn't even occurred to her to switch on the entrance light."

Arturito got out of the cab and stretched out his hand: it was smooth, his deep-pink nails delicate and narrow like those of a newborn baby. He bowed deeply to kiss Teleca's glove.

"My beautiful Teleca."

"She has left the street in the dark."

Arturito's nails fluttered like fireflies.

"Light, give me light!"

"Please, Arturito, try to understand. Your mother takes care of everything for you. You don't realize how difficult it is to deal with these people."

Arturito's mouth, pink as his nails, twisted with irritation. His smile – his normally full lips that stood out for being so full – tightened into a cruel grimace.

"Teleca, dear, get reading. I'll call you tomorrow; I want to know your opinion."

With a brusque gesture, Teleca put the key in the door, caught a glimpse of Arturito tapping the shoulders of the taxi driver with the handle of his stick, and the car went off.

Teleca climbed the steps in big strides. "Lupe! Lupe! What's been happening?" She reached the second floor. "Lupe!" Went into the ironing room and the kitchen. Where on earth can this Indian woman be? Snoring in her room, I imagine. "Lupe! Did anyone call?" She stopped on the landing of the servants' stairway. "Lupe! Lupeeee!" She had never gone into her room on the roof. It was one of her principles. Perhaps she's in the library polishing the furniture. I doubt it, but she might be. She went in that direction full of hope. The bookshelves shone as Teleca opened the door and followed the ray of light with her eyes. In the darkness they acquired shades of a Vermeer, their suspended corners outlining the air. Ridges glinted, the rounded arm of a chair appeared out of the shadow, smooth and electric like the curving back of a cat. Time polishes, molds, and destroys. "It's very stuffy in here. Not only is she not here, but she hasn't ventured in here for a long time, in spite of my orders. What a filthy woman." She climbed upstairs again and went flying through the rooms. "Lupe, Lupe!" Once more at the foot of the service stairs, she cupped her hands and shouted, "Lupe!" She had never taken so long to answer. Disgusting Indian, she has abused my patience.

Teleca decided to go up to her room. As her heels hit the iron steps, she felt she was climbing into space. At the top she heard the dripping of a tank. No sheets were to be seen hanging on the roof. The door of the room flew open; there was no lock. The smell of feet and sweat imprisoned there hit her and she opened her mouth, gasping for air. The room was empty.

"She must have gone out to buy bread," Teleca tried to reassure herself. "But she never goes out at this time of the night. Besides, I have told her not to leave the house when she is alone. That's it, I must sack her; she is making me ill."

She walked around the bare room, looked in vain for the cardboard boxes in which Lupe had brought her belongings. Opened the wardrobe. Empty. The air blew in from the windows without curtains. "She has left."

Teleca had to accept the evidence. She went downstairs without knowing what she was doing and made straight for her bedroom. The key was there. She had not taken anything. Her jewels were there. For a while she stood in the center of the room, arms to the side, wondering what next. Not a single noise in the house. Worked up by all that running about and her emotional state, Teleca fell prey to her fear. She tried to gather courage. "It's for the better; after all I had decided to get rid of her. She was always going against me. This way we avoided a scene. I'd had enough of her flat nose. Traitor. All's well that ends well, isn't that what they say? Traitor. It's the best thing that could have happened."

She started to take her hat off, turned on the bedside lamp, and closed the curtains one by one. A rosy light spread around. Rich people's houses always have a rosy light. In a slight state of euphoria she went into the kitchen to get her jug of water for the night. "Now I am going to read *Les Faux Monnayeurs*. I had decided not to eat tonight, anyway, so what does it matter?" She went around the house, walked into the lounge, crossed the dining room. Her heels echoed in all directions like castanets, to the right, to the left, turn around . . . "I am like a teacher of flamenco dancing," Teleca thought, indulging herself. She brought two vases of flowers out on to the landing. "Filthy woman, the water is green. She never changed it. Lupe! Lupe! I must be going mad. She did me a real favor by "clearing off," to use their ugly slang." Facing the wardrobe, she tried to hang her coat. "Lupe, where are the hangers, the wooden one for my coat? I must be plain delirious talking to that wretched woman. Tomorrow I will wear my lacquer-red dress; it's the color that most suits me. Has that stupid woman thrown my shoes away? Lupe, Lupe!" Exhausted, she collapsed on the carpet with her face in her hands. Only then she noticed that her cheeks were wet. Could she have been crying all this time? She stifled a sob. "Lupe, dear! The best thing to do is to take a tranquilizer, go to bed, and tomorrow I will find somebody else." Teleca used to forget about her body – it was so slight – but now it was burning, echoing, amplifying all the sounds inside it. Stretching her arms she pulled back the heavy damask bedspread, which had previously been on her parents' bed. Slowly and with great care. And there lying on the snow-white sheet level with the embroidered *A* and *S* that wound around the family shield she saw the turd, an enormous crap, in spiraling circles, an awesome rainbow of green, coffee, turquoise, yellow, and ash-gray, still warm. In the midst of the silence the smell began to rise.

When years later Teleca told Arturito about it – she had not said a word to anyone before – he said it was not possible; the Indians were not vulgar, had no scatological or coprophiliac tendencies. They would never do anything of the kind. This was not within their pattern of behavior, absolutely not, as any anthropologist with expertise in indigenous customs would confirm. Lupe must have let in some drunken delivery man, a poor devil whom city life had reduced to scum, and together they might have conceived this wicked joke. . . . After all, looking at it without prejudice, it was a childish thing to do. Stubbornly shrugging her shoulders and frowning in disagreement, Teleca insisted, "No, no. It was Lupe's."

Translated from the Spanish by Psiche Hughes

Aunt Mariana

It was very difficult for Aunt Mariana to understand what life had dealt her. She said "life" to give some kind of name to the mountain of coincidences that had settled on her bit by bit, although the total might have presented itself like a fulminating tragedy, in the exhausted condition she had to contend with each morning.

To all the world, including her mother, almost all her friends, and her mother's friends – not to mention her mother-in-law, her sisters-in-law, the members of the Rotary Club, Monsignor Figueroa, and even the municipal president – she was a lucky woman. She had married an upright man who was engaged in the common good, the depository of 90 percent of the modernizing plans and activities of social solidarity that Puebla society counted on in the 1940s. She was the famous wife of a famous man, the smiling companion of an illustrious citizen, doe most beloved and respected of all the women who attended mass on Sundays. Her husband was entirely as handsome as Maximilian of Hapsburg, as elegant as Prince Philip, as generous as Saint Francis, and as prudent as the provincial of the Jesuits. As if that were not enough, he was rich like the landowners of yesteryear and a good investor like the Lebanese of today.

Aunt Mariana's situation was such that she could live gratefully and happily all the days of her life. And it may never have been otherwise if, as only she knew, she had not crossed paths with the immense pain of spying on happiness. Such idiocy could have happened only to her. She who had proposed so much to live in peace, why did she have to let herself get in the way of war? She would never stop regretting it, as though one could regret something one did not choose. Because the truth is that the vortex inserted itself deep into her, the way cooking aromas from the kitchen enter the whole house, the way the unforeseeable stabbing pain of a toothache comes on and stays. And she fell in love, she fell in love, she fell in love.

Overnight, she lost the smooth tranquility with which she used to awaken to dress the children and let herself be undressed by her husband. She lost the slow lust with which she drank her juice and the pleasure she felt sitting for half an hour to plan the dinner menus every day. She lost the patience with which she listened to her impertinent sister-in-law, the desire to spend an entire afternoon baking pastries, the ability to sink, smiling, into the tedious sameness of the family dinners. She lost the peace that her pregnant bellies rocked and the hot, generous sleep that overtook her body at night. She lost the discreet voice and ecstatic silences with which she surrounded her husband's opinions and plans.

Instead, she acquired the terrible talent for forgetting everything, from keys to names. She became as inattentive as a deaf student and as difficult as people who are ill advised by indifference. She no longer had a purpose. She who thought herself made to solve minor problems and who bet she'd been created merely to fulfill the desires of others, she who enjoyed herself noiselessly with the plants and the aquarium, the unfolded socks and the orderly boxes!

Suddenly she lived in the chaos that comes from permanent excitement, in the jumble of words that hides an enormous fear, jumping for joy in the face of unhappiness with the feverish obsession of those who are obsessed by a single cause. She asked herself constantly how this could have happened to her. She could not believe that the recently met body of a man she had never anticipated might have put her in that state of confusion.

"I hate it," she said, and after saying so, devoted herself to the pitiful care of her nails and hair, to exercises to shrink her waist, and to plucking out the down on her legs, hair by hair, with eye-brow tweezers.

She bought herself the smoothest-ever silk underclothes and surprised her husband with a collection of shiny briefs, she who had spent her life touting the virtues of cotton!

"Who can I tell?" she murmured while walking in the garden or trying to water the plants in the corridor. For the first time in her life, she had used up the large sum of money her husband put away for her each month in his wardrobe safe. She had bought three dresses in the same week, when she used to debut one each month so as not to appear ostentatious. And she had gone to the jeweler for a long chain of twisted gold whose price scandalized her.

"I am crazy," she told herself, using the qualifier she always used to disqualify those who did not agree with her. And it was true that she did not agree with herself. To whom would it occur to fall in love with her? What folly! Nevertheless, she let herself reach the foolish precipice of needing someone. Because she had an insubordinate need for that man who, in contrast to her husband, spoke very little, did not explain his silence, and had ir-replaceable hands. For these alone it was worth risking all her days to be dead. Because dead she would be if her craziness were known. Even though her husband was as good to her as he was to everyone else, he would not save her from facing the collective lynching. All the adorers of her adorable husband would burn her alive in the atrium of the cathedral or in the public square.

When she came to this conclusion, she kept her eyes on the infinite and, little by little, started feeling the guilt leave her body, to be replaced by an enormous fear. Sometimes she spent hours prisoner of the intense heat that would destroy her, hearing even her girlfriends' voices call her "whore" and "ingrate." Then, as if she'd had a celestial premonition, a smile opened in the middle of her tear-stained face, and she covered her arms with bracelets and her neck with perfumes before going to hide herself in the joy she had not used up yet.

Aunt Mariana's lover was a gentle, silent man. He made love to her without hurry or orders, as though he and Mariana were equals. Then he asked: "Tell me something."

So Mariana told him about the children's colds, the menus, her forgetfulness, and, with total precision, every one of the things that had happened to her since their last meeting. She made him laugh until his whole body recovered the boisterous frolics of a twenty-year-old.

"I rightfully dream they are burning me in the middle of the street. I deserve it," Aunt Mariana murmured to herself, shaking off a piece of straw from a stable in Chipilo. The refrigerator in her house was always stocked with the cheeses she went to look for in that village, full of flies and blond peasants, descendants of the first Italian sowers of anything in Mexico. Sometimes she thought that her grandfather might have approved of her proclivity for a man who could have been born like him in the hills of Piedmont. She returned while it was still daylight, in her auto without a chauffeur.

Upon coming home one afternoon, she passed her husband's Mercedes-Benz. It was the only Mercedes in Puebla, and she was sure she saw two heads inside when she watched it pass. But when it stopped in front of her car, the only head she saw was the upright one of her husband, returning alone from the ranch in Matamoros.

"How clear is my conscience?" Aunt Mariana asked herself, and followed her husband's car on the highway.

They traveled one car behind the other the whole way, until arriving at the entrance to the city. One turned right and the other left, both waving their hands out the car window to spy good-bye, in agreement that at seven in the evening each still had obligations to take care of alone.

Aunt Mariana thought that her children would be just about ready to request a snack, and that she never left them alone at that hour. Regardless, guilt hit her suddenly as she thought of her hardworking spouse, capable of spending the day alone among the melon and tomato growers he visited as far away as Matamoros on Thursdays, only to go back to the store and the Rotary Club, without allowing himself the slightest break. She decided to turn around and catch up with him at that moment to tell him of the evil that had overtaken her heart. In two minutes she had caught up with the cruising Mercedes containing her husband's elegant head. With trembling hands and tears welling in her eyes she neared his car, feeling that she would put her final force in the hand that waved, calling to him. Her entire expression begged forgiveness before she even opened her mouth. Then she saw the beautiful head of a woman reclining on the seat, very close to her husband's legs. And for the first time in a very long while she felt relief; pain turned into surprise, and then surprise into peace.

For years the city talked about the sweetness with which Aunt Mariana had endured the romance between her husband and Amelia Berumen. What no one could ever understand was how not even during those months of grief did she interrupt her absurd habit of going all the way to Chipilo to buy the weekly cheeses.

Translated from the Spanish by Amy Schildhouse Greenburg

Procession of Love

"You should punish the woman as well," he said, sobbing.

The prison cell was no bigger than his body. They had handcuffed him and told him to remain on his knees. Until he confessed.

"Yes, it is love, but you don't know it."

By the end of the night he drank some milk, lapping like a cat. Filled himself up with the liquid as if sucking the breasts of an acquiescent animal. I am not free yet, he thought, using his last remaining strength. He yearned for freedom, to be able to sing and say, "I have been so much in love as to forget God."

This image excited him; the voluptuous idea of being stronger than the divine through the power of the flesh. The stone walls were etched with screams and tears, scored by fingernails and forks. Even after they untied him during the day, they did not allow him any movement. Forbidden to straighten his body, he was forced to retain a position of submission. His limited space was his punishment, so their looks were saying. He didn't mind and said to them, "I have to love, to conform with nature."

His daring, as well as his tears, inspired laughter. "Confess!" shouted the guards. But they could not get anything out of him. Only the occasional smattering of words that no one could understand and that would eventually contaminate the world.

They strove to unfold the man's secret text. To get at some truth. Yet no sooner did the fury and violence of his screams seem to show signs of his weakening than a look or a gesture or more incomprehensible words proved the contrary, that he would forever remain deaf to their interrogation. Food was turning into a solid mass in his stomach. It would go on nourishing him. That is what he explained to them one happy morning.

The man's despair seemed to proclaim, I am free from fear as if a gigantic mountain dared to shelter me. They even asked him how he would react if they brought in the woman.

"With teeth and nails," was his dark answer.

They feared such defiance. That when the two came face to face, love would pronounce itself in such terms that no one would ever perform the same gestures without feeling disgraced and revolted by their own emotions. This man made any other love impossible, as the judge had said in sentencing him. That is why the authorities, faced with his transgressive behavior and the necessity of its punishment, had to move with caution.

On the fifth day, his flesh was still swelling, though his handcuffs remained almost permanently closed. In the end, they felt so insulted by his look that they unbound him. Delirium. The cell had now become a paradise, and the man who had been made to lie so close to the ground adopted the strangest attitudes. The prison wardens were moved by his exuberant display of happiness. Who could remain insensitive watching such irrational behavior, the delight manifested by this strange animal? They had never seen a being like this one. Perhaps he was the first in the whole world. He had to be punished.

The woman, though rebelling, realized that she would never see him again; these were the laws of the city. Day and night she paced her cell in the city convent, which, unlike his, was quite spacious. During the trial, the judge had not dared to look at her. He explained to the public that he felt too much repulsion for a creature who had invented a love that nobody on earth could replicate – although, if only out of contempt, some people had tried to. This woman and this man had awoken the most inexplicable feelings in all of them. It was enough to observe them to feel the shame, the unforgiving longing of paradise lost.

When their violent passion was unveiled, they were denounced. It was generally suspected that the man and the woman's expressions of love had transgressed all established ways. They even smiled when arrested, as if obeying some overpowering command. Living in a cave or a royal hall made no difference. And when asked about their secret strength, they became silent in their pride. Eliminating the presence of all others, they looked resolutely at the ground, which now seemed to them insignificant.

There was evidence that they had not abandoned the room in which they had been loving each other for over four hundred days. Yet their skin was the color of a fresh apple. Only one voice in the community had protested against their arbitrary arrest. What if they had exaggerated? Isn't this how love is known?

The city had dragged them to trial in shackles. Faced with their enemies, they behaved like animals hating each other, but they were profoundly happy to meet. They could not bear to be apart. To the people in the community, everything they did appeared indecent, endowed with mystery. The unrecognizable objects found in their house – the rare perfumes, the wall hangings of skins of animals never seen before – were especially disturbing. Perhaps, as well as being lovers, they indulged in witchcraft.

After the first month in prison, sadness began to take its toll on the man's health. But still they asked him to confess, "What kind of love were they practicing that the whole city felt insulted and ashamed by it?"

The priest spoke to the woman: "Was your act of love always honest, or did you offend the Lord?"

The woman lying on the ground looked up at the ceiling and said, "Ah, love . . ." and lost herself in the fragile but innocent world of delirium.

The priest fled and later confessed, "We are running a great risk of being but shadows."

When they threatened him with the death of the woman if he

didn't talk, the man gouged his eyes out with a fork, and the bleeding pulp caused great fear. Not even death moves a creature like him. And they ran away and asked the priest to take care of him and of his incurable blindness. They were afraid; in the presence of the man, they also saw only shadows. They told the woman what he had done. She did not condemn it; a soft smile inundated her face, and she said, "I knew he was strong, but I did not know he was invincible."

She sang all day as if to celebrate the man's blindness. People said that his useless heroism made it impossible to go on making love. They felt remorseful, their bodies vulnerable, and now condemned as well to this darkness. For the sun had become frail, its pale light hardly entering their houses in the early hours of the morning, as if night had hardly ended.

People tried everything to free themselves from the lovers' influence. Couples spent whole days shut in their rooms to be like them even when boredom threatened, until at last they could not stand each other and began to shout, "Free the woman and the man."

It was not because they felt pity, not after a whole year, but because they wanted to think of them as free. The judge succumbed to public opinion, which was becoming more insistent by the hour.

On the appointed day the woman came out of the convent accompanied by a small group of people. The man dragged himself along the walls and was let loose in the prison yard. The crowds looked forward to the encounter; they had not told him that as well as blindness and sudden freedom, he would now have to face the woman again. They had kept this from him, for the moment when they would see them bound together in each other's arms, the only possible happiness.

The woman went toward the man and looked at him as if he were a stone. In spite of his blindness, the man walked in her direction, perhaps following her smell. They stood like statues of salt, then started walking, without saying a word. She in front, clicking her shoes so that he, whose hearing had heightened in the last few months, could follow without her help.

The crowds resented such a display of indifference. It was dignity, said the man who had always defended them. All the same, he trusted that eventually they would signal the intensity of their feelings by some gesture that the onlookers would promptly register. So they began to follow them wherever they went. When the couple stopped, the people would stay up all night to catch them by surprise. They could not accept that their behavior obeyed different rules, that some deep-seated harmony held them and turned them into images of each other.

From that day on, the lovers never touched or spoke a single word. The woman did not try to help him, though he might need it; nor did the man, whose sense of pride had reached new heights, extend a begging hand. From time to time, as the road surface changed, or as she was exhausted by the walk and the poverty of their existence, the sound of her shoes became softer, and the man fell to the ground groping among the stones. The woman stood then, watching, her expressionless face showing no pain or desire to help, until the man got up again, unaided, with no sign of anguish, for he understood that she acted for their salvation.

They never tried to escape from the community to indulge in the love that they had defended for so long. Day after day they offered the city the same vision of their simple life, until the people who followed them to discover the origin of their strength and cunning despaired at the desolate sight. It was not just that of the woman's and the man's bodies being consumed, as if shut in their room in long episodes of love, fed only by powerful memories that, delving into the past, carried them unerringly into the present. Rather, it was the desolation of the entire city now unable to resist them.

They lived off fruits and roots. Anything people put on the road for them to eat was left to rot. And whenever a stranger touched them, agony seemed to strike their bodies as if they were still in prison. But the birds surrounded them and animals licked their legs.

Not for a moment did the memory of the punishment leave them. Nor did they hide behind trees or in caves. In case people thought that any form of communication or gesture of love might pass between them, even for a moment, they sought open areas, squares, wide streets. The procession behind them was witness to the modesty of their behavior. At times people asked how long they would last; were they following them for nothing? Others wondered, what kind of love is this that seems to devour and annihilates us?

One day the man was given a stick to defend himself in his darkness. He threw it far away, but those who followed him began to use a stick or staff to lean on. They wanted to share in their sacrifice, and some went to the extreme of hanging from trees, staying there for hours, their mouths parched, their muscles in agony.

The couple, on the other hand, lay on rocks, but she no longer looked at him, especially later in the parade. Not only had she perfected a system of noises to prevent him from hurting himself; she had also begun to imitate him, to become his accomplice, to assimilate his blindness, and would walk back to meet the spiky bushes that had scratched him so her body could also know his suffering. The tearing of their limbs became more and more apparent, and the city, following this endless parade, were pained at the sight of such bleeding.

Nobody could bear their proud defiance any longer. The two faces, daily proclaiming the pleasure of a secret, hidden anger, never registered lust. Until one day the mayor said:

"They have won. Let's stop following them. If you wish, we can execute them."

The city refused: that kind of love would have to die sometime. They were now ready to champion any kind of stigma. Following them, they visited streets, fields, hunted butterflies and other wonderful things – the sense of the divine – even though the man and the woman continued to live in total obscurity.

Translated from the Portuguese by Psiche Hughes

Santa Catalina, Arequipa

For Albrecht Götz von Olenhusen

I have been working in this monastery full-time since they restored it, and all my life centers around it. I know every corner, every nook, and I can tell the age of the various plants of honeysuckle. At times I lovingly caress its rough walls, which I fancy are full of secrets, a silent chronicle of centuries. I could find my way without hesitation in any part of this labyrinth of narrow streets, small squares, and cells, even with my eyes shut. Far from being bored, I am wondering what it will be like to live without them after the first of May when I shall leave for a permanent vacation. Nobody knows yet, of course, and they will believe that I am coming back until I don't show up on the first of June.

This convent is more familiar to me than the little house of my childhood in a poor village on the Cordillera, or the two rooms I rent in Cortaderas, now my own home since I successfully repaid all my debts and wrenched myself free from my godmother, free as the wind.

I know by heart how many jars of water were used by the servants for the nuns' laundry and how, during the course of the day, the shade of these walls changes – right up to five in the evening when the light here in Arequipa takes on a blue tinge, which is exhilarating, a great contrast to the whiteness of the porous volcanic stone. The locals stop to admire the light, wherever they happen to be. They congratulate themselves – even those accustomed to grumble at the start of the day about the frequent showers of sleet – delighted by their extraordinary luck in living here. And the

lines of the beloved waltz whip through their minds. White city /
eternally blue sky / pure sun / mountains of my home.

During these past eight years, as part of my work, I must have
walked up and down the Courtyard of the Orange Trees and the
Calle Granada thousands and thousands of times. And explained
to the tourists, just as many times, the changes introduced two
centuries ago by Mother San Román de la Vega. And an equal
number of times looked at her deathbed portrait, which I now
manage to identify easily, even in the semidarkness: her habit as
Mother Superior, her eyelids dripping like wet rags, her penitent,
crossed hands. I have enjoyed the special acoustics of the Pinacoteca during the rare musical events and have witnessed the occasional splendid banquets given in the old refectory and in the
Courtyard of the Three Crosses. I have learned to appreciate the
hourly ringing of the bells, which can be heard better from the
alcoves in Calle Sevilla. Those very sounds that had tortured me at
first, like a broken lament, a nauseating racket.

I no longer ask myself whether it is a kind of perversion to vol-
untarily shut yourself between these walls just to pray, without a
man or anybody else. And to imprison your maid as well to die
here, having come on foot under the weight of an enormous cross
from as far as Bolivia. I have been more concerned with the ad-
vantages of living on my own, without ever returning to my village. To wear city clothes, lose the accent that betrays my origins,
adopt my own way of speaking, and not show excessive pleasure
at the large tips the tourists give me. And above all, not to make
peace with my godmother, Eloisa, to break off all contact.

Punctual, courteous, and proud, I haven't missed a day's work; I
have recommended to everybody the cream of rose petals to heal
scars and the marzipan and orange cakes. I have started washing
myself with parsley soap, also made by the nuns in their cloisters
and assiduously sold through the revolving window on the Calle
Bolívar or at the convent shop. Whenever invited by the tourists, I

have also drunk numerous passion fruit juices and maté teas in the old granary, now transformed into a cafeteria. And many times I have encouraged them to climb to the roofs to admire the perfection of the domes and view the profile of the sleeping Indian of Pichú-Pichú, the serenity of the volcano El Misti, and the imposing shape of the Chachani, perpetually bathed in variable snow: Eternally blue sky / pure sunshine / mountains of my home.

I couldn't have chosen a better place to kill Esteban.

Esteban is the name I gave him after we had been together for a few months. And "together" is also a manner of speaking, but let me proceed step by step. After I broke loose from my godmother's control and her plans to turn me into a housemaid, I set myself to learn languages with determination and at great cost in order to get this permanent job, which more than one professional guide longs for. I took pains to learn and understand the respective cultures and mentalities of the tourists so as to be able to tell them all about the monastery. I therefore found it rather commonplace to have a fiancé called Steve, not so much because my name, Laura Zárraga, is so resoundingly Latin and Basque, but because he was born in La Havana. Even if Miami lies in between.

Although, thinking back, God knows how much truth there was in the story of Miami – or of Cuba – apart from the accent.

Steve Cordero, to crown it all.

"Stif" I found hard to say. Esteban Cordero sounds much better, and that's that.

So I told him when he came back, "I don't like Steve. I'll call you Esteban."

"As you prefer, my love. It doesn't change a thing. You call me whatever you want, as you wish."

'Fiancé' is another matter: the drama starts just when I discover that Esteban, Steve Cordero to be exact . . . and that was only a month after, when I broached the subject, that he had said:

"Why are you so anxious Laura, my love? If I told you we're

127

going to get married, we will get married. Only you've got to be patient. How can you be so distrustful?"

This gave some moral support to my tummy, which had begun to grow after three years of wild lovemaking, a totally new and exclusive experience for me. And I told him with joy in my voice, my radiant eyes reaching for the sky. An attempt to control the flood of happy images that flooded my soul.

But all the caresses and kisses remained ridiculously poised on my lips. Esteban's face had suddenly changed: a stony pallor fell on his tan "à la dolce vita." After a few solemn moments, he spoke in a lighter tone, though unable to disguise his disapproval.

"But my love, you're moving too fast. This is a matter for later on. For when we are comfortably settled, don't you think? Right now we are living from hand to mouth. And my dream is to be able to keep you in style."

"I have set aside some savings, if that is what worries you. There is no need for you, I mean to say, I could easily . . ."

"I don't think so, my girl. Rushing such matters always brings bad luck. Everything in its time and place. It might even make us stop wanting to see each other!"

He managed to speak of something else with that voice that made me tingle all over and with the confidence of one who knows he is loved, unconditionally adored. He spoke of other things, which convinced me that the subject was closed.

But when you carry the subject in your tummy, moving and swelling your hips and breasts, it is quite another matter. The cells plot in iron complicity. Instinct takes hold of the whole organism with magnetic force. A woman cannot explain where it is coming from as she examines herself in the mirror. A twenty-eight-year-old woman who, during the last three years, has been kept breathing by the arbitrary visits of the man she loves: "I'm sorry, next month I can't. I'm not guiding any group, but the following month, yes, we shall be together. Aren't you the love of my life?" And the woman is left looking at the receiver, and she doesn't break it because she is too civilized. Anyway, I'm not trying to put together the script for a soap opera. All I need to do is to lift this horrible weight off me. Having to keep silent for the rest of my life, never able to hear a "You did the right thing, Laura, he deserved it."

I shall slip away from this novice's cell, which is still in the process of restoration, sure of being able to keep absolute silence at whatever price. How many times entering the cloisters have I read it, and shall go on reading it until the end of the month, carved on the thick wall like a traffic signal: SILENCE.

She might have preferred to forego this deathbed portrait: ninety years old, all expression gone from her face, not even one of devotion; a face covered in faint moles, like a map marked at random after a cataclysm. It was hard work to get the portrait of Mother San Román de la Vega down. I had to push it out with the corner of the kneeler, balancing myself like a trapeze artist on the end of her bed. My wrist got caught in cobwebs, and I felt quite sick. But I needed her company, her presence, to give me courage and to lift me over the abyss. Something tangible and banal, like the heavy bags under her eyes, or her platypus nose, to transmit her contempt for the human body, for our enslavement to beauty, and to redirect me toward the noble question of the soul. Something finally to help me to come to terms with the extent of the sepulchral silence that awaits me.

Needless to say, I haven't slept all night, with little snakes frolicking all over my tummy, now the seat of childish pranks. I am ready: in a few minutes, as the sun rises, I'll go to the large cell of Mother San Román de la Vega in Calle Segovia and replace the portrait, looking at it in full light; the heavy moustache and the colorless skin. Then I'll return, my lungs full of oxygen and somewhat restored, to my hiding place in the novices' quarters. And when the cleaners have finished with their dusters and brooms, and the gate and ticket office are open to the public at nine o'clock, I will walk calmly, freshly made up and in control of my speech, to the cafeteria as if I weren't feeling faint, terrified of Laura Zárraga. As if I were just coming from Cortaderas, fancying a delicious breakfast: papaya juice, a meat pie, buttermilk with dark-brown honey. As if I had never killed Esteban.

I sit in the kiosk next to the ticket office and listen with evident pleasure to my colleagues narrating yesterday's anecdotes and details of their private lives until I am allotted my first tourist group of the day. We go through the monastery in one and a half to two hours, in English, French, or Italian, stopping in the Calle Granada as little as possible: no desire to take a turn and find myself face to face with the place in which it all happened. I know that for years to come it will not cross the mind of any guide to do so. And at the end of this month I am due to go on vacation, just as my pregnancy will begin to show – not that they would ever suspect – and I'll go abroad with my savings. I'll disappear from the face of the earth without telling anybody that I shall never come back. And that there are two of us, and we are going very far away. Who will care, anyway, in this city where I don't belong?

The monastery will take on one of the many qualified experienced guides who are hanging around waiting for the job. Having tired of ringing the bell, they will break down the doors of my two little rooms in Cortaderas to collect the monthly rent. They will find no trace of me, assuming that they may look for one. I have worked it all out. I obtained my passport last week. I shall go to Puno by train, from there to La Paz by coach, and fly to Belgium. Of the many addresses left me by tourists, and the cards and photos some of them have sent me, and from all their warm invitations, I have chosen a childless couple of psychologists from Amberes whom I accompanied to buy chocolates from La Ibérica and eat a chili stew in Los Tres Sillares. I believe they will give me shelter until I find a position. Once out of the country, little will matter if, in the annual fumigation in October, or some time later, they find the corpse. I won't even hear about it and, with any luck, they may never find it. The little passage behind Calle Toledo is so often forgotten.

Either way, by then I shall be over seven months' pregnant, busy knitting babies' clothes and going swimming every day. In fact, being no less vile and callous than Esteban is a strengthening thought. It gives me the feeling of having operated with justice, without the need to buy the relative and questioning silence of third parties. With a shattered heart but a safe belly and a head well screwed on in its place. With the assurance that everything else is secondary.

Exempt from guilt and cleanhanded. With that kind of contempt that manifests itself in the refined elegance with which one plans a criminal act step by step. Criminal, but just. For nobody can get it out of my head that the wedding took place only because of the banknotes and the glamour. In order to lead a life of leisure. For Esteban, that idiot, did love me.

And he knew how to release my juices. And extract their fruit.

He turned up here when the Monastery of Santa Catalina had been open to the public for some time and had acquired international fame because of the unique beauty of its architecture. His job was to lead a group of Arizona farmers, a fairly coarse lot, unfamiliar with the habits of the cloisters. He looked at us all in the kiosk and chose me to guide him and his gringos through the convent. It seemed that fate wanted us to exchange a quick kiss that very afternoon – excited under that "eternal blue sky" – and on one of those rooftops, while the farmers amused themselves throwing coins in the wishing well. I, who had always guarded my distance and silently criticized the chance affairs with foreigners of my colleagues. I, who did not know how to use my tongue. What followed, until Esteban flew to Lima – to return from there, I imagine, to the United States – is not very original, in spite of my virginity, nor is the frequent use we made of rum and sheets.

Whenever I thought of my behavior, once I acquired a taste for it, I said to myself, that's how things should be.

There was not much originality either in his visits every three, five, or six weeks with different groups of tourists. To say that I fell in love with him, down to my marrow, is not to speak the whole truth. Nor would it be correct to describe my spectacular and patient dedication in terms of self-denial. I just gave myself without fear, prejudice, or reservation. Without a single lie. And I believed everything he said from A to Z because it was such a pleasure to listen to him.

It was like music. Always with a cigar in his mouth, and his coquettish trick of feigning ignorance of anything boring. He made fun of the eccentricities of his friends, described unusual aspects of Florida, hummed old-fashioned boleros, and eventually described, in plausible detail, our future together as strung together in the romances of Barbara Cartland, the kind my godmother collects. In between the music of one or another story, he possessed me. I now think of it as a recipe – the kind of which one dares not change the ingredients for fear of a surprise.

If only I had missed seeing the photo in that magazine – with such a triumphant look. He never thought that a poor, self-made tourist guide from the provinces, determined to improve her lot, with little time available and great contempt for those frivolous gossip magazines, would all the same leaf through this one in the doctor's waiting room. And the irony is that I had gone to the doctor because of my "condition."

Of course, we don't know whether the lucky groom, at the height of his happiness, realized that he was posing for the romantic press and not just for the family album. We don't know what version had been fed to the family or to the brand new Señora Cordero, former widow of Santisteban.

I mean to say, the brand new widow of Cordero, ex-widow of Santisteban. When she sees that her second spouse does not show up, she will become jealous and begin to doubt him. After a few days, she will hate him, analyze his reasons for their wedding, consult her lawyers. She will set up an order to search for him in the whole of Lima and bring him back in whatever state he is found. The following week she will deny her age and that she has dyed her hair. Wracked by despair, having lost all faith in her psychoanalyst, she will spend a fortune in just a couple of months to establish that all is in vain: her husband, such a good-looker, and so capable in bed, is nowhere to be found; the earth has swallowed him up. Which is not so very different from being buried under the volcanic stone that will guard the smell of his putrefying corpse like a secret.

I don't know what tricks Steve used to escape from the little palace in Monterrico and to come and see me. And since she, the widow Ana Rosa, obviously knows nothing about me, her searches don't worry me.

I didn't make him come to ask for explanations. I am from a rugged land where people act rather than talk, people born to work like mules. And rather vengeful types.

"We, the Zárragas," my mother managed to tell me before she died of consumption, "are bastards, as poor as church mice. This you must know. But you must also be proud to your core. And do all you can to escape from this filth and poverty."

I was too young to understand and looked at her in confusion.

"Don't allow yourself to be stepped upon or trampled down, no matter what," she added. "And, above all, beware of men. There are many swines around. And they lie and trick to get their own way. Take good care, my child."

I didn't make him come to blackmail him either, as my godmother would surely have advised me to do.

When I met him at the airport, I wasn't even sure he would be there. He had phoned after a silence of five weeks to tell me that he was in Lima and would be able to organize a trip by the end of the month with a group of pensioners from Oregon. And that the situation was not easy until June, when the high season started. But he had taken advantage of the gap to do a lot of studying. No question about my condition. I still had in front of me the page that, a couple of weeks before, I had torn out of *Lima Linda* in the doctor's waiting room. I had kept it all this time to poison my life and my dream. So I gave him this ultimatum in a loving voice, dripping with insincerity.

"Esteban, you promised that you would come once without tourists especially for me. I want you to come now."

"But I've just told you . . ."

"Make it a Wednesday, which is my free day. I'll come and meet you."

And I put the receiver down, quickly set fire to the page from the magazine, and went walking along the Avenida Bolognesi, looking at the river.

In fact, at midday, as I was watching his plane landing, I sincerely hoped he would not be there, as had happened on the previous Wednesday. After his last call, when I came back from my walk, I had disconnected the phone: my decision was made.

He got off first, tall, his chestnut curly hair longer than usual, his skin more bronzed than ever, and a cigar ready between his fingers. He was smiling. New clothes, of better quality, loafers rather than sport shoes, a leather suitcase instead of a backpack. I noticed that he had put on a little weight and that it suited him. And how accustomed I was to the call of his body.

But I had a job to do. It was the only way to get justice, and it had been hard to make that decision. I had invited him to come in order to kill him. And he – he was too vain and too pleased with his lot even to imagine it.

As always, he was happy to see me. I am well aware that my delicate mestizo features – my flowing blue-black hair, and all the bedroom tricks I learned to his great advantage – drive him out of his mind. So happy to see me that he didn't even ask the reason for the urgency of my invitation. He bought me a bunch of carnations and hugged me with greater tenderness than ever before. But he made the mistake of not asking any sort of question about my belly. That could still have disarmed me, but he made the fatal mistake of hiding his secret from me. He must not have thought that news from his social circle – that things were not as they were, or God knows what – that news of such an extravagant wedding would appear in the papers.

It pains me to think of his long agony. I killed him as a matter of principle, not just for pleasure. Seeing him stuffed inside that space like molten metal in a prepared mold, I realized how useless volume can be.

I admit I would have preferred a sudden death; it must have felt like an eternity to be running out of air and the ability to deceive, when it is too late and his well-built body is turning into a compact mass enclosed in a shell no bigger than itself. Made to measure almost, unable to make a single useful movement. The tips of his fingers scratching against the splintering door, covered in blood as he pushes, gathering all his strength with his shoulders, his knees and the entire frame of his body and head, unable to accept that these centuries-old blocks and iron hinges can support tons of weight. It pains me to think of his long agony but, as I said, I could not run any risk.

We took a taxi from the airport to Cortaderas; our embraces were silent, full of anguish on my part but no less satisfying and pleasurable for him, after which I suggested that we go into town on foot. It seemed grotesque to walk arm in arm, to cross the Avenida Bolognesi, stopping over the Grau Bridge to look at the river, as one seeks the other's face in the reflection, for proof that he is still there. And it seemed grotesque to let him hold me by the waist when, just over seven weeks before, the widow Ana Rosa Martelada, daughter of the owners of the famous supermarket chain that had entered the country in direct competition with the small shopkeepers, was joined in marriage to Steve Cordero, the handsome sales promoter from the United States, "who has been residing in our capital for the last few years. The groom's mother, a Puerto Rican, came especially for the wedding from San Juan. The bride's parents held an exquisite banquet in the Hotel Crillón for five hundred guests. The happy couple left for their honeymoon in Buenos Aires, Asunción, and Rio de Janeiro. Upon their return they will establish themselves in their new house in Monterrico. . . ." I certainly do have a very good memory for some pieces of writing.

To think that on my way to the doctor I had just posted him a letter, as I do every Thursday or Friday, to the Chameleon Travel Agency in some district of Lima, an agency whose existence I had never bothered to confirm.

"You'd better write to me in Lima, my love," he told me at the start. "From the Chameleon they send everything to Miami by courier, and I'll hear from you before you write. I am no letter-writer myself, as you know. I am a numbers man. I prefer to call you on the telephone."

The compass that determines the direction of our feelings did not make me hate the widow Martelada, not exactly ugly, though a little overripe in spite of the bronze tinge of her well cared for hair. And only ten or twelve years older than Esteban . . .

The compass that determines the direction of our feelings made me concentrate on my obsessive need to punish him.

What did I know of Esteban, whose name, after all, I had invented? What did I find out after a love affair of three years? That he lived in Florida. That he adored me. That he accompanied tourists to Peru whenever possible to finance his postgraduate studies. That he was only happy with me and missed me all the time and was as faithful as a dog. That he would soon finish his exams and then we would go and live (married of course, what do you think?) where they offered him a permanent job. That he loved me more and more for being so good and pretty, hard-working and faithful. That his parents knew about us and congratulated him for being so lucky, because there aren't many more good girls left, and sent me their love. That he loved me forever but, for the moment, he had to concentrate on his studies. It was devilish what one had to learn in order to get a Ph.D. from the gringos.

But he would obtain it before reaching thirty because he adored me. It was just a question of patience, just a few more months, only one semester. The most important thing of all was – and I should never forget it – he adored me. . . .

And I was by nature the kind of person who believed it all. One who does not ask for documents, who does not insist on seeing where things have actually occurred, who accepts the rules of the game of life no matter how unfavorable. And by nature one who writes more letters than she will receive, who is easily betrayed. Who dedicates herself to someone with complete abandon. No matter where he lives. No matter when he turns up.

The afternoon light yesterday was so brilliant, even he remarked on it: "What's happening to your city? It's as if it dressed itself up just for us."

He did not hear my threat: "It's not my city. And don't trust it too much or you might be stuck here like a limpet."

There was no reason why he should understand, but he gave a polite, hollow laugh. We crossed San Francisco Park. The jacaranda flowers scattered on the ground increased my agitation. I had made him come in order to kill him, but nobody, I believe, is a born killer. As we turned the corner of Santa Catalina, on our way to the Plaza de Armas, I suggested we go into the convent alone for once. There, where we first met.

Having a bad conscience, he could not say no to any request of mine. Surprisingly silent, we followed the well-known route: the turnstiles, the light shining through the Huamanga stones, the roof terraces. The miniature cell of the martyred nun who had come on foot from Bolivia. We crossed the larger cloisters to enter the Pinacoteca, just as five struck. I was sweating and hoping for any kind of portent that would frighten us away: an earthquake, the sound of a fire alarm.

We looked at the paintings of the School of Cuzco as if we had never seen them. We were almost on the point of signing the visitors' book when I gently pulled at his sleeve. Instead of going out through the turnstile that led to the kiosk, I took him to the confessionals near the age-old doorway in the patio of the three crosses.

"Sit down," I said. "You must be exhausted. It is time to confess your sins."

A last-minute trick, from my subconscious. An open metaphor, begging him to tell me all in minute detail, giving me some sort of explanation, no matter how despicable. A morbid desire to forgive him and forgive him, to embrace him forever in my forgiveness: to make him stay with me. Or to run away wherever he wanted. Together.

He did not give any sign, only that look of the passer-by who doesn't notice, to which I had become so accustomed. His seat on the eleven o'clock flight the following morning was confirmed. Had he ever stayed in Arequipa more than twenty-four hours with the tourists?

"What ideas you have, my girl," he said. "What whims. How come you have suddenly acquired the father confessor's complex? Careful, it can be quite morbid. All that's missing is for you to take a photo of me sitting right here."

Ideas, whims, complexes. It was 5:40 and not a soul was left in the tourist area of the monastery, which is separated from the nuns' residence by a stone wall and a set of ruins. I knew only too well that old Hermenegildo locked the gates and the big door at half past five on the dot and went to drink a glass of anise with the cobbler at the corner of Ugarte. I also knew that the remaining hordes of visitors left the only fortified convent in the world at 5:25, at the latest, and that the ticket office's padlock latched at a quarter to five.

We turned into Calle Toledo and made for the passage that, as tourist guides, we normally omit from our tour because it only has two penitence cells, identical to those found at the entrance of Calle Sevilla, which are more than adequate exemplars with which to frighten the tourists. I still wanted to kiss him in order to forget, to be left with some scraps of his fictional life, which still belonged to me. Wasn't he there with me at that moment, dying to get back to my bedroom and to fill me with his desire and enthusiasm?

I still wanted to pull his thick eyebrows together to read deeper inside him. To shout that his tales and his tricks did not matter as long as he loved the baby, gave him his attention and his name. I wanted to say this and more, wipe all out and start afresh. But I carried so much hatred in my body: I could feel it bubbling in my veins in the tension of my collarbone, the tautness of my muscles. I led him instead into that hollow, looked at him a while and said to him in an aggressive voice, which sounded strange, even to me.

"I bet you can't fit into such a small space."

Frightened, I thought how a challenge is the one trap that always catches men.

Esteban said, "You don't think, my girl, that just because I am a good-looking boy I can't bend like a rubber doll. I am very flexible, my little Laura, especially when you ask me."

And these, paradoxically, were his last words.

I was quick, very quick.

His long thighs forced him into a fetal position. His knees seemed to stop the beating of his heart. As a parody, he folded his arms and placed his hands in that contrite attitude of Mother San Román de la Vega on her deathbed.

Before falling into the temptation to forgive him, faced with his caramel-brown eyes, the bounce of his curls, I gave a mighty push on the old splintery stone door and turned the centuries-old key twice with an ability I never would have suspected I had.

I knew how well that nook of penitence was sealed, and that in the dark ages of history the nuns of Santa Catalina – not much taller than four foot ten – would sit and lock themselves in there for something like half an hour, to sweat out their penance to the last drop. That is why the keys were always available by the door. This is what I used to explain to the tourists when showing them the cubicles at the entrance to Calle Sevilla. I also knew that Esteban suffered from claustrophobia, though he would never show it in public. And I knew that his smoker's voice was not very loud.

I knew that I had taken into account all unforeseeable and remote circumstances. As in a meticulous game, locked inside, he formed the last piece of a jigsaw puzzle or a masterpiece. In there, his icy sweat would impregnate the fissures of the historic building, part of the patrimony of humankind. In there, the white stone would soak in his smell and spread it throughout its pores as a discreet accomplice.

I walked stealthily up to the Plaza Córdoba, afraid of breaking down, turning it all into a sick joke, of shamefully giving in to a sense of pity. The evening light bathed the wall of the three wings of the refectory and the ochre arches of Calle Sevilla.

Of course I was pouring sweat, and the rusty key burned my hand. I looked at it with some respect. It was like the keys drawn in language textbooks, not like our modern keys. The prototype, the kind people imagine every day to be one of St Peter's: big, solid, black, and heavy.

I was amazed by my lack of pity, my craftiness, my success, and swiftly threw the key into the wishing well, with my back to it, as part of the ritual. Wishing with all my heart that I would never let my secret out.

Santa Catalina, Arequipa

The key fell quietly, as I watched its descent among the hundreds of tourists' coins until it drowned in their midst. Drowned like Esteban's screams forever embedded in that space which, come to think of it, seemed made to measure.

Each time I walk by Calle Toledo for the rest of the month, I shall think of him in profile, doubled up and docile. I can't curse him enough for being so stupid, for not taking the trouble to ensure that events in his private life would not reach my ears. I'll call the baby Esteban, and I'll let his curly hair grow down to his neck. And when he asks for his daddy, I will tell him that he died of pneumonia during a very strange, unfortunate journey he embarked upon during the worst season and without listening to my advice.

Translated from the Spanish by Psiche Hughes

Impossible Story

They were left alone. Laura suddenly felt tired. She sat on the edge of the bed to take her shoes off; made of stiff leather, they seemed to him more rigid than wooden clogs. "I'm going to put some music on," she said to him. "You'll love it. Wait a minute." She went into the bathroom and shut the door. He remained alone, wondering at everything he saw: the transparent vase on the bedside table, the table itself, the shelves full of books, when the sound of music hit him, a blow that Montezuma could never have imagined, like a coup de grâce yet full of joy, something that deafened him at first and then filled him with emotion. What music was that? When Laura came out of the bathroom, he asked her, "What am I listening to?" "There are many instruments," she explained, "interpreting the music written by a man called Vivaldi. I put it in this box where it is being played for you because Vivaldi wrote an opera with your name. He made the music, which is the sound you can hear, to honor you, many years ago, much closer to the time when the captain of La Malinche landed here than to our present day." And she thinks, How could Vivaldi have ever imagined that one day Montezuma would hear it on tape? Never! While Montezuma wonders what artifices Laura employed to make so many musicians play such strange sounds. What kind of sounds are they? What does one hear in them?

But Montezuma is not thinking. At this point he no longer thinks. He no longer wonders "what?" and "how?" Does not say, "It can't be" or "I'm a Mexica Indian. I live differently from these people who have invented other ways of being." He says nothing, remembers nothing as if what he sees might affect his being, invade his body, enter his pores, consume him. No, not consume him. Montezuma is there present, watching, conscious without speaking or forming a judgment. As if he did not have a body, only eyes or rather, as if instead of having eyes and a head, he were just a body that explores and sees. That is the only word I can think of: see. He does not order things, or explain them, yet he misses nothing. At lightning speed he has invented within himself a way to survive, this new way of being. Not for one moment does he say to himself: "I'm Montezuma, miraculously reborn in the same geographical space where once stood the great Tenochtitlán." He never thinks of what is happening, not because he shuts his eyes but because he opens them more and more. It is as if abolishing his original vision of life and death, of the universe and nothingness, he arises a new being made up of wonder and observation. There he is Montezuma watching, feeling.

Why did Laura once again take him in hand like a child? She led him to the bathroom and placed him in front of the toilet. "Have a pee in there, pass water, if you prefer to call it that, and I'll be back." And she shut the door. Standing alone by the lavatory, he undid the knot of his pants and pissed. An endless stream that could not be just the result of the chocolate drunk that morning; an ancestral flow of urine cut off (as the result of a wound?) on the day of his death and which by some stupid biological error had stayed in his body. Perhaps that was why he had been sent back to earth with his entire body, to release in this lavatory the urine he was not meant to keep in his death. With slow and ceremonial movements he once again tied up his pants, and she came back, flushed the chain, and let the water flow from two taps into the pink tile bathtub, mixing the two jets until it was full of warm water. She undressed him and helped him to get in, chatting all the time, "What a lovely bath, just for you, to calm you down and see whether you change that expression of yours and look more at ease." Montezuma got inside the bath and relaxed in the warm clear water and watched her pour a liquid in it, something that turned into bluish bubbles. Then she rubbed him with a very smooth sponge, rinsed him with clear water from the handheld hose, and helped him out of the bath, wrapping him in a soft towel.

Standing in front of him she undressed and gave herself a quick cold shower, to wake me up and get rid of this hangover.

She then wrapped herself in a towel, got out of the bathroom, opened the door to the bedroom, and laid on the bed on top of the damp towel. Then she threw it aside and went naked under the covers. He watched her, let his towel slip down on the wet bathroom floor, and went naked toward the bed. Laura lifted the covers to let him lie beside her. What happened then had nothing to do with the power of desire. It would be foolish to think so; how could he desire her or she desire him? At first it was as if their bodies had stumbled, missed a step, and the sheer clumsiness had made them fall by each other's side and embrace. But after the first move, clumsy and accidental as it was, turning over at the same time from their different positions, they allowed their bodies to fall into each other's arms as if they were alien objects.

The result was of such comfort – not entirely devoid of desire – and of such relief that they could no longer let go. They were releasing each other from their suffering, their painful situation. For her, the meaningless condition of a young woman full of life, at the end of the twentieth century, living in a city once the greatest and most beautiful in the world now the most crowded, the most populated, and perhaps the most insane of them all. For him the uncomfortable feeling of waking up centuries after his death in the very place where his city stood, recognizing nothing except the skeletons of his temples. Nestling between two clean sheets, a light eiderdown filled with goose feathers and two pillows with embroidered edges also of white cotton, Laura and Montezuma inexplicably – and this is not an author's nonsense, because if you are to consider the act you'd soon call it incredible and even idiotic, but that's what happened, and what am I to do besides just say so – Laura and Montezuma inexplicably copulated, fucked, became man and wife. You choose the term, this is your privilege, name as you like the act they performed and which I am hurrying to re-count before these pages be irremediably condemned (the story is pretty well finished) to come to an end.

For a while they seemed not to be moving, or rather to be both trotting at the same rhythm, her two hands placed on his hips pushing him away from her ever so lightly – yet such a separation between their two skins – until his body fell again hard and strong, deeper into the hollow that Laura's thighs could not hold back. For a long while they seemed not to be moving, identical as they were in their movements (one-two, one-two, their repeated comings and goings), a canvas to which the skilled artist added final touches: drops of sweat here and there, hair tossed away, muscles relaxing in a uniform, precise rhythm.

For a while they were firm as a statue balanced by the comings and goings of the wind, still, impeccable in the exasperation of the approaching climax. Every part of their body was pleasure, their teeth and ears, their nails and their flickering eyes. But they did not, could not know this because they were standing at the edge of the place where everybody gets lost. They did not know that they were feeling pleasure, as if they were never to come out of its un-conscious state.

A new element intrudes like a dagger, which tears the perfection of the canvas; the voice of Laura scoring the picture they are form-ing, perfect, divine in their perfection within that image which nobody could understand just by looking, a drawing of flesh and spirit (if you could distinguish one from the other), an incom-prehensible work perfected by a passion without name or explanation, whose only meaning lies there in that moment torn by Laura's voice, which says in a tone too feeble to be imagined,

"I am coming, come with me!"

And after this voice, so new in her mouth, Laura's body dissolves like smoke arising from a burning corpse, like steam from water before disappearing into dispersed particles, which no longer remember or know that they had been water, that they had belonged to it.

And him? The same thing happens to him. What remains of him on the bed is his atrocious dejection, the white yolks of his semen, the senseless grayish thick stain, left behind, while he returns to the air, the wisdom of rocks and water, forgetting, perhaps forever, the uncomfortable verticality of the human body. All pleasure at last without distinction, turned into complete surrender where not time or language or custom watch over one's actions, like the fattening of victims, measuring the warm fragile immensity of man, then to crash it, blunting out all flexibility, against the blind reality of the individual.

He dispersed into minute unidentifiable particles, in the fins of a fish, the bark of a tree, the bed of a river; wind and fire where the air that surrounds the earth ceases to exist. No memory, no city, immensely wise in his lack of knowledge, without wondering whether or not he would once again be called to duty or even whether he ever was. His consciousness lost in minimal deaf and blind fragments, finally exempt from pain, struggle, battles, and wars, from the vacuum and the absence of being, powerful or not, man or woman, free or slave in all the meanings of the word, like a nail in the wind, being nowhere, made of nothing, with no truths, altogether good, more good than bread, wise as a stone but without the misfortune of intelligence.

Translated from the Spanish by Psiche Hughes

Spick and Span

It all started with the wind – when Margarita told her husband about the wind. He had not yet shut the front door of his house, arm stretched downward toward the handle, eyes gazing into his wife's eyes. It was as if he could remain forever in this pose. But then he howled. It was astonishing. For a few seconds they remained motionless, looking at each other as if needing to be reassured by the other about what had happened. Until Margarita broke the spell. Casually, almost tenderly, as if nothing had happened, she rested her hand on her husband's arm to keep her balance and, with the other, gently pushed the door shut, while, with her right foot poised on a soft cloth, she wiped from the floor the specks of dust that had just come in.

"How was your day, darling?" she asked.

And she asked it less out of curiosity than to reestablish normality (given the circumstances she did not expect an answer, nor did she get one). This routine evening question was like a coded message: Everything is okay, regardless. Nothing has happened, nothing new can happen.

Having finished wiping the floor, she let go of her husband's arm. He walked away rapidly toward the bedroom, and she felt as if a butterfly, held by its wings, had escaped her fingers. He had not wiped his feet as he walked out of the room. This meant that he was furious. He was obviously overreacting. After all, it was not as if she had asked him to throw himself naked from the obelisk. But she said nothing. Using her own floor cloths, she wiped off his shoe marks. And decided not to go into the bedroom. On the verge of doing so, she turned toward the kitchen. It was better not to add fuel to the fire. Later on, she would find the right moment to talk about the wind.

Supper was ready. At first she had thought of preparing steak and fries – his favorite meal – despite its being Wednesday, but then had changed her mind. The greasy smell impregnates the cupboards, the walls, even your will to live. If left from Wednesday until the following Monday, when she did a thorough cleaning of the kitchen, the grease would penetrate to the very pores of everything and settle there forever. So she had taken a quiche out of the freezer and stuck it in the oven. She was setting the table when she heard her husband go into the bathroom. A minute later, the cheerful streaming of the shower resounded through the house: a good omen.

The time had come to go into the bedroom. As soon as she opened the door, Margarita could see that he had left his clothes all over the place. She brushed his jacket and his trousers, and hung them up, gathered his shirt and socks, and knocked at the bathroom door.

"I'm coming in, darling," she said softly.

He was humming and did not answer.

Margarita took away his underwear and added them to the dirty pile. She washed the lot with enthusiasm. As she turned the tap off, he had started on "When You Are in Love." The storm had passed.

The following morning at breakfast, however, half in jest, as if not to give too much importance to the scene of the previous night, Margarita referred to the wind. No big deal, she admitted, but it didn't take much effort, did it? It was not something that would in any way complicate his life. All she was asking was that, when the wind blew from the north, he come in through the back door, which faced south, and, when it blew from the south, from the front door, which faced north. He might like to call it her little whim, but he could not imagine how it would help her. No matter how much she swept and polished, the floor was always covered with dirt when there was a north wind. Of course, he could come in from whichever door he fancied when the wind blew from the east or west, not to mention when there was no wind at all.

"There you are, my wild one, no need to make such a fuss." She laughed mischievously.

He raised himself to his feet as if to make an important speech, hawked loudly, almost with pleasure. Then, bending slightly forward, he spat on the floor, recovered his upright position and, with measured steps, walked out of the kitchen.

Margarita was left looking at that ring of spittle shining in the light of the morning sun, as one might look at some minute creature from another planet sitting undisturbed on the kitchen floor.

A door closed and opened, the walls shook, his footsteps crossed the house, another door closed with a bang. Margarita's brain only barely registered the sounds. The whole of her was concentrated on that small ringlet on the floor. Source of infection. This expression, which had just flicked through her mind, expanded and flooded it like a wave. In trains and buses, when someone coughs, a spray of invisible drops carries around thousands of germs. How many germs must there be in? . . . Millions and millions of germs stirred, gamboled, and floated over the red tile floor. Margarita grabbed the first object at hand: a napkin. She got on her knees and rubbed the floor vigorously. Useless. No matter how much she rubbed, the sticky circle stood out like a stigma. Squashed germs dragged themselves along like amoebas. Margarita put the napkin on the table and fetched a sponge soaked in detergent. She wiped the mosaic with it and poured a bucket of water on top. As she was about to dry the floor, a thought paralyzed her: was she mad? She had used a napkin to . . . my God! When a napkin is normally used to wipe one's lips! She picked it up by a corner and looked at it with terror. What to do now? Washing it would not be enough. She put a saucepan of water on the stove and threw the napkin inside.

As she was wiping the table with disinfectant (the napkin had rested for some time on it), the telephone rang. She went to answer it and, as soon as she entered the bedroom, she sensed something unusual. Something that seemed to oppress her deeply inside. Only when she put the phone down and opened the wardrobe door did she understand its cause: all his clothes were gone, of that she was sure. Very well. He had left. Marvelous. Was she going to cry? No, she was not going to cry. Was she going to tear her hair out and hit her head on the wall? Certainly not, neither tear her hair out nor hit her head on the wall. You don't bemoan the loss of a man. Men are so untidy, so dirty; they cut bread on the table, leave their footprints on the floor, open doors against the wind, spit on the ground. A woman can't keep her house clean – nor her body. She just can't keep her body clean; at night men turn into animals, drooling . . . their breath, their sweat, their semen, the disgusting secretions of love. How could an all-powerful God make love such a mucky business? Filling the bodies of his children with so much dirt, the world with so much filth? Now, however, never again. Never again in her house. Margarita stripped the bed, pulled the curtains off the rails, lifted the carpets, shook the cushions, tidied up the lace cloths. She rubbed, shook, and swept until the knuckles of her hands turned red and her arms cramped. She washed the walls, waxed the floor, polished the metals. The saucepans shone so much they reflected the sun, and the hanging crystals took on a brilliant sparkle. The porcelain shepherdesses were bathed like darling children, the wood was buffed, wardrobes perfumed, the stones bleached white. The alabaster glistened. At seven in the evening she shook the brush in the rubbish bin, as an artist adds his signature at last to a long dreamt-of painting.

Then she breathed in deeply the air impregnated with the smell of polish. Slowly and with satisfaction she looked around. She took in the splendor, savored the whiteness, tasted the transparent clarity, noticed that specks of dust had fallen out of the rubbish bin into which she had shaken the brush. She swept it into the pan and emptied the pan into the bin. She shook the brush once again but with greater care this time not to drop a single speck. She put the brush away in the cupboard and was about to do the same with the dustpan when a thought struck her: people tend to be casual with dustpans, they use them to gather all kinds of rubbish and never think that some of it must remain attached to their surface. So she decided to clean the pan. She used detergent and a little brush. The water in the sink turned quite dark. Margarita washed it out, but a mark, something like a black rim, remained at the bottom. She wiped it with a soapy cloth, rinsed the sink and washed the cloth. Then she remembered the brush. She washed it and made the sink dirty again. She rubbed it with the cloth but realized that, if she was to clean the cloth in the sink, this would become an endless process. Best to burn the cloth. She dried it first with the hairdryer and then went out and set fire to it. As she came back in, there came a gust of north wind that inevitably blew some of the ashes into the living room.

Better not to use the brush now that it was clean. She took a cloth (she could always burn it) and some polish. But it didn't work. The floor changed color. She rubbed and polished some more around the area. It was useless.

By five in the morning, all the floors had been scraped, but a reddish dust floated in the air, covered the furniture, and stuck to the skirting boards. Margarita opened the windows, swept the floor (eventually she would find time to wash the brush and, at worst, she could throw it away), and had just finished washing the skirting boards when she noticed that some of the water had spilled on the parquet. Discouraged, she looked at the damp patches. She felt weak. Judging by the light, it must be about seven in the morning. She decided to leave it till later; with any luck, she wouldn't have to scrape the floors again. She lay on the bed without undressing (must remember to change the sheets again) and fell asleep immediately, while the damp patches spread, became slimy, stretched their tentacles, got hold of her, trapped her in a swamp into which she sank deeper and deeper. She woke with a start – she had hardly slept half an hour – got up, and went to check the damp patches. They were drying up but remained visible. She scraped the area again, but it remained a different color. Feeling slightly faint, she fell to the ground. When she half-opened her eyes, she glimpsed those whitish streaks and sighed. She realized that she had not eaten anything in the last twenty-four hours. She got up and went into the kitchen: a hot meal would make her feel better, but it would mean dirtying the saucepans. She opened the fridge and was about to grab an apple when a horrible thought struck her. She had not swept the dust from the second sanding and the windows were open. She withdrew her hand abruptly from the fridge door and dropped a box of eggs. She watched the yellow slimy pool spread and thought that she might cry. Must not. Everything in its right time. First sweep the dust off. The kitchen floor would have its turn later; nothing like sticking to routine. She picked up pan and brush and went into the living room. As she was about to start sweeping, she noticed the soles of her shoes. They were dirty and had traced intermittent tracks of egg fluid on the parquet. Looking at herself with her tools in hand, Margarita almost burst into laughter. "The dust from the scraping," she murmured, "the dust from the scraping." She remembered that she still had not eaten, dropped the pan and the broom, and went straight into the kitchen.

The apple was in the middle of the yellow puddle. Margarita picked it up and bit into it greedily, knowing at once that it was ridiculous not to prepare a hot meal: everything was dirty anyway. She put the grill on, peeled the potatoes. It was fun to watch the spiraling strips of peel fall and soak into the yolks and whites on the floor, now that everything was dirty and she would have to clean it all later, anyway. She put the steak under the grill and poured some oil in the frying pan. The fatty meat crisped up with joy, the fries sizzled. Margarita remembered that she had forgotten to open the kitchen window. But it was too late. The greasy vapor had already penetrated the pores of everything, her own included; had impregnated her clothes, her hair; had thickened the air. Margarita breathed in deeply. The smell of meat, of frying, entered her nostrils, drowned her, drove her mad with pleasure.

People can become clumsy when they are impatient. As Margarita drained the chips, some of the oil spilled on the floor. With a furtive foot, she spread it around. The steak fell as she removed it from the grill. She picked it up. Its proximity, its touch, that wonderful aroma of roasted meat inebriated her. She couldn't help digging her teeth into it before putting it on the plate.

She attacked her food with ferocity, put the dishes in the sink but did not wash them. She was very sleepy. The time would come to wash everything. She turned on the tap to let the water run and made for the bedroom. But she didn't go that far. While still in the kitchen, she slipped on the greasy sole of her shoes and fell. She felt very comfortable on the floor, anyway, and rested her head on the tiles and went to sleep. She was awakened by the water. Scattered with oily drops, it crept across the kitchen, meandered in narrow channels along the joints of the tiles, and, in diminishing streams, headed toward the dining room. Margarita had a bit of a headache. She dipped her hand in the water to bathe her temples. She turned, stuck her tongue out as far as possible, and managed to drink some. She felt better now. She had a cramp in her tummy but lacked the strength to go to the toilet. Everything was pretty mucky anyway.

Must not soil your little dress. Margarita was six years old and had to keep her little dress clean. And her knees. She had to be very careful not to dirty her knees. Until in the evening someone called, "Bath time," and she'd run to the bottom of the garden, roll in the earth, rub it into her hair, her nails, her ears, to make every crevice of her body feel dirty. Then she'd soak in the purifying bath, the bath that would remove all grime from Margarita's body and leave her as radiantly white as a new bud. Do marguerites have buds, Mama? She felt an unspeakable sensation of well-being. Moved a little away from where she had been lying and wanted to laugh. Pointing at something near her, she said, Poo-poo! Her finger dipped in it voluptuously and she wrote her name on the floor: Margarita. But it wasn't so noticeable on the red tiles. Effortlessly now, she stood up and wrote on the wall: Shit. And signed it: Margarita. Then she drew a big heart around the two words. A draught of air on her back made her shiver. The wind. Coming through the open windows, it brought in all the dust from the street and the grime of the world, which stuck to the walls, her signature, her heart; mingled with the water on the dining-room floor, entered her nose, her ears, her eyes, and dirtied her little dress.

Two days later on a bright sunny day, when the sky was a flaw-less blue and the birds were singing, Margarita's husband stopped in front of a flower stall.

"Marguerites," he told the stall-keeper. "The whitest you have. Lots of them."

And with this huge bunch he walked toward the house. Before putting the key in the lock, he made a funny gesture, played a little game, a game of love, which an affectionate wife, hiding behind the blinds in expectation, would much appreciate. He licked his index finger and, lifting it in the air, observed the direction of the wind: it was from the north. So the man, obedient and happily anticipating the unique flavor of reconciliation, went to the back of the house. Whistling a cheerful song, he opened the door. A gentle splashing came gurgling from the kitchen.

Translated from the Spanish by Psiche Hughes

End of the Millennium

Him

He has so many possibilities: he can blow his fortune in one night in Paris or New York, or he can go to Fiji, the first place in the whole world where the third millennium will start. It is up to him. He will not be able to find a room in any hotel, but that does not matter; he does not need one. He has been looking it up, exploring it on the Internet, and knows all the prices, packages, and tricks. He can dispose of more than seventeen thousand dollars without it having an impact on his family – they do not even know it exists – and this sum should be more than enough.

In front of him there are photos of himself; what is not there is a mirror: he even shaves by memory. Little by little, since he has been living alone, he has eliminated all reflecting surfaces from his apartment. In the photos on his desk – he was thirty then – he looks very handsome. Now, at more than twice that age, he has considerably less hair, white, of course, which he can see on the comb, although he tries to use it as little as possible. He writes a lot, but what he writes is a distorted autobiography, somewhat apocryphal, of that blessed age of thirty, and he has decided to remain frozen at that happy stage of his life, fixed in time. He re-solved to do this three years ago and, being thirty, has become his new persona for the many temporary relationships he has formed on the Internet. All beautiful and crisp – unless they also lie – some even interesting. With these he persists the longest, meeting them every night on the screen of his computer, until some white hair or a wrinkle inevitably appears in his recent photos. To keep up with his persona, he must become a year older, and this he can-not bear. So he breaks the relationship outright. He gets rid of this blind date and starts new ones, painstakingly, till he finds another young woman who, like the previous one, may for a time succeed in freeing him of his anguish.

After his triple bypass, things became very difficult; he can't bear to think of it. To think of the time when he became unable to answer women's invitation, to brandish his truth, for his truth had become like rubber and no longer responded to the rush of his blood. Then he had a modem installed and turned over a new page.

Today, however, everything is different. Today, time is on the point of starting afresh, we are on the verge of a new century, a new millennium, and even virtual reality is about to betray him: on the first of January, zero hour, all computers might go mad, screens fade out, the world come to an end. Y2K is how those who know describe it in apocalyptic North American jargon. Faced with such Armageddon, he has the right to be once again the man he was at thirty, hair blowing in the wind, his now washed-out green eyes shining once more. Just once. He made this decision suddenly, but now he wants to plan it carefully and without haste.

He sends a final e-mail to his children in Mexico wishing them all happiness, much more than they deserve. They went to live in Mexico City 7,400 feet above sea level, knowing perfectly well that he could never visit them at that altitude, the two buggers, his daughter in particular who, by moving there, managed to alienate him from his grandchildren. They no longer matter. Nor does his ex-wife, who never understood him, certainly not his need to express himself, his manhood, whenever he went off with some broad or some nurse – one and the same thing – his need to give free rein to all that wonderful energy that used to bubble inside him and does no longer. How his wife must have laughed in the last three years; this is her revenge – poetic justice, she must have thought, the idiot – when the operation had unexpected side effects. He no longer wants to hear her voice nowadays, not even get in touch with her by e-mail. Screw her. She would only bore him, telling him once more to reopen the clinic, that his patients have great confidence in him, need him. With a bit of luck they will all be dead by now, he had answered, but she would not be put off. It is not that you are irreplaceable, it is just that you are a good doctor, she had retorted without taking offense. How can he be a good doctor if he can't cure himself? Good or bad, what matters now is that there's no longer any response in him, and better not think about it. . . .

Except that now thinking is the only vital activity left to him: thinking, planning. Dust off the old prescriptions, consult the file of his online romances. The old and the new ones. Which might be better? Who might be telling the truth? He has no time to waste exploring the possibilities of RL. In real life – he prefers the acronym – as if the other life were not in its way also real, him shining eternally young at thirty, with sparkling eyes and boundless energy. I am going to fuck you this way and that, and do this and that to you, as he now writes to some of those sluts who, from a distant computer, tease and excite him. There I am coming, a long eruption of burning white lava, gushing all over you, and similar bravado, while they, the idiots, are lapping it up with pleasure, not knowing the damage they are doing him.

They are all the same, yet it would not be a bad idea to fuck one of them.

But he is no longer thirty, as he has assured all of those gals, not even in the remotest corner of his heart is he thirty, because his heart crashed one morning in his clinic, and he was taken straight to the operating room – and now this. He has tried to restore that thirty-year-old corner of his battered heart with thousands of words, but he is running out of them, out of words, out of time. When midnight strikes on the last day of this month of December, nothing will be the same. The century, which saw him revel in memorable fucks, will have gone, the computer screen will have eclipsed, and so will the photos of him at thirty. The handsome hunk he had managed to bring to life on remote monitors will lose what little substance it may have ever had. Not even the memory of some verbal orgies that had nourished him over those years of electronic communication will survive. The nourishment is finished. He's finished, as they say.

They may all be the same, good-for-nothing sluts, but he has his moral code and cannot do a thing like this to any of them. Innocently they float in cyberspace, as one who wallows in a rumpled bed. No, he couldn't do a thing like this to any of them, even without considering the subsequent mess. How easy it would be to trace him through his Internet address. And then the family would intervene, his children would come down from Mexico to see him when it was too late. Not to mention his ex-wife and her idiotic cousins, who never gave him credit; the revelations they would make to the press. I can't have any of that. And of course Johnny, trying everything possible to comfort my wife, always meddling in things, he who said from the start, "You hate women 'cause you can't get it up any more." With what pleasure he had sent him to hell once and for all, this so-called former best friend. I don't hate women, I love them, and, for this, I hate them.

No point in becoming sentimental now. This is the moment to take action. Wipe the dust off the old prescription pad, the old suits, although in this heat he can't think of suits; shave – by memory – the neck and part of his face; a trim little beard might look good, can't tell; he neither wants nor can look at himself: no mirrors. Must wait till he goes out, till he starts walking again, farther than the supermarket, as far as the bank, and farther. Until he puts a cover on the computer, the monitor, the keyboard, and printer. Black, in mourning.

Her

Nurse, intelligent, and tart. How can these three attributes be reconciled? Yet they define her. That is what she repeats to her image in the mirror: "You are a nurse, intelligent, and a tart."

Nurse and *tart* are concrete terms but, as for being intelligent, it is a matter of personal appreciation. What's more, her present situation might even disprove it. Was it intelligent to come to Comodoro Rivadavia, this wretched windswept town, just to change her life? Only in so far as she achieved her aim and changed her life. There was no other motive for her do so, nobody pursued her; she had always been irreproachable, objective, and efficient in her work, just as they had taught her; never allowed herself to become soft, to linger on with a more pathetic case. She had given equal attention to all patients, just what was strictly necessary, medically required. But her job had let her down; she had been made redundant after an employment record of thirty faultless years. The senior surgeon, having appointed her his personal assistant, his right hand, as he had often told her, suddenly became left-handed, turned around, and kicked her out.

In her new work, if this can be called work, she adopted the same attitude as in the old one: equally irreproachable, efficient, and unbiased. Never too tender, although at times she did allow herself a little more time, especially if she had an inkling of pleasure, even though it might be only an inkling.

At her age she couldn't ask for more. Actually it is not so: she is at an age when she should ask for everything, because at last she knows what she wants, except that nobody will give it to her. It would be like calling out into space. Better to be silent. It is her greatest skill. Tonight, once more, as during the last few months, she will confront the harsh winds along streets she does not recognize, having to close her eyes to keep the dust out. She will turn the revolving doors of Garby's, breathing with relief the still air saturated with the smell of men, which invites her to open her eyes again. At Garby's, penetration is limited to words. Somebody will sit by her side at the counter and tell her the story of his life, the drama of it, because there is no point in telling it unless it is a drama. She will listen with great attention, professionally, doing

161

her best to suggest to this potential client the absolute need to pass from verbal to vaginal penetration, the only lucrative one for her. It is a life like any other, she tells herself, another aspect of her previous life, the one that, having sucked her dry, spat her out on these shores.

Once inside Garby's, she opens her eyes but does not look at the man who, on this occasion, sits by her side. Nor allows him to look at her too closely. It does not flatter her, being over fifty, although she knows she carries her age well. Her flesh is firm and her smile youthful. This she developed here, as she had never had occasion for it in her previous profession; her smile is younger than she is.

With the senior surgeon in Rosario, in that faraway place, now so remote in time, her occasional smile was limited to the corners of her mouth. And he, one happy morning, made her redundant, claiming it was a question of budget, and took on an inexperienced assistant with no seniority, that is to say, much younger and more appetizing. She complained and protested so much that now she has no intention of opening her mouth. Only as a duty in her new job she opens it and then she knows how to suck and drink in, just as she drinks in the words of the client who, for her, is never a man or an individual, just a client. A being. Damn him, she curses on more than one occasion, although the man she really should curse a million times is the bloody surgeon.

There, in the past, in another sort of hell.

At the Airport

"You are the only arrival, you know. They have all left in the last few days, all gone to the capital, or where their families are to celebrate. Nobody wants to stay in Comodoro to see what kind of year 2000 the wind is bringing them. The town council had planned fireworks over the sea, but they decided against it; the fireworks would go off before reaching the necessary height. Even the bureaucrats went away; they will have a better time in Trelew or in Rawson, so they say. No room for color here, only this sort of gray, the gray of this gray area. I don't know why you came here, today of all days, to end the century."

He had not sat down to drink his whiskey on the rocks in order to chat with the barman. As it was, however, it suited him because he needed some information.

"I just had to come for work," he answered rapidly. "I couldn't help it. But I wonder where I can find some girls. I don't want to spend New Year's alone."

"If you work for the oil company, you'll be all right. They put you up in good hotels. But then you must go to the Imperial; there are first-class chicks there, real stunners. Just ask my friend at the bar, and he'll introduce you to the best. Tell him that Truman sent you."

"Any other places?"

"It's very private at the Imperial, but it's all a question of taste and money. You could also go to the Tom-Tom, quite a classy haunt, dim lights, and all the gimmicks. Alfonso runs it and can advise you about other forms of entertainment, if you care for that."

"Anywhere else?"

"Yes, there's Garby's, but I wouldn't recommend it. The girls there are, how can I put it, getting on."

He asked for another whiskey and sat at the bar in silence without drinking. He was adjusting himself to being there, in the cold. He had decided to come to Comodoro Rivadavia because of the temperature. No desire to go frying in the heat, losing all his energy. There were no more flights left for Europe or the States, and anyway the journey was too long, with a change of language and the possibilities of power cuts. Too much effort for his very simple plan. The idea of a rough sea had appealed to him, but from the plane he had not seen any water, only an ocean of dunes and oil wells.

He came out of the airport as night began to fall. There was enough time to do the rounds.

He decided to start from the bottom, got into a taxi, and asked for Garby's. He wanted to keep a low profile, remain entirely anonymous. His watch showed December 30, 8:30 P.M. The plan would gradually follow its course, without his having to think too much about it.

At Garby's, he asked for another whiskey with lots of soda. Must go slowly. In the bag by his side there was a great deal of money, more than enough for good measure. Glass in hand, he began to look around. In actual fact there wasn't much choice, and they all did look a bit worn. He would have to go on to more welcoming sites, although the atmosphere here was not unfriendly, on the contrary, there was a kind of homely warmth, God knows why. Some details of the décor brought back memories from his child-hood, scenes from cowboy films. That's what it was; like being in a saloon. He likes the idea; he is happy to postpone his departure. He is in no hurry. Adds more soda to his glass, turns around on his stool and looks for – he is not sure for what. The woman at the counter two stools away from him seems to have guessed what he had not been able to formulate – was not allowed to – and offers him a packet of cigarettes. He looks at it, flustered; he has not smoked in three years, but now he could really do with one, and it doesn't matter any more. Stretching over the counter he says, "Thank you, thank you very much, just what I needed." She is not smoking and does not answer. She just touches his hand slightly, taking the packet back, and breaks into a smile, an unusual smile, a smile that comes from somewhere else. Not submissive or se-ductive. A smile all of its own, with its identity and sense of in-dependence. She is fulfilled and has a way of being, in this place and at this moment, that wipes out all other possibilities. This suits him, does him good. Perhaps it is contagious. He looks at her straight in the eyes as if asking for a light, not that of a match – the barman has already obliged – a light that sparks in her, that flashes out of her eyes, a woman's eyes on fire, fixed on the man's, which begin to recover their old iridescent splendor.

The Encounter

They are sitting at a table. Things have happened at Garby's – in this saloon time has passed, but not at their table. Here, glasses have been filled over and over again, and the fire in their eyes has not been extinguished. She feels there is no need to get him into bed, that they are happy here. We are happy here, he thinks, I can stay here another twenty-four hours, and then there is still a lot of time, and I don't want to move. He has asked for more cigarettes, but it is just to recapture the feel of her hand, because the cigarette remains in the ashtray, and its blue smoke rises slowly in Garby's blue silence. Outside the wind roars: it sounds like a hungry wild animal. "I have been a hungry wild animal," he says, as if speaking to himself. She understands it to be so and lets it drop. Hungry for whom? With whom? She does not ask. Resting her head on her hand, she does not move, does not talk; just that sudden surprising smile, and he knows that she is present, there, for him. She would like to know, but she is not curious. "When I was thirty," he says, and it is as if he said "now." At thirty, that is now. She realizes that he is touching on a very delicate point. It is for this that she has come all that long way from the hospital in Rosario without stopping, without drawing a single breath. She lets him be and at the same time she would like to hit him, squash him under her feet like a cockroach. This man has no right, no right whatsoever, to come and dig up the past. He leans back on the chair and scrutinizes her from head to toe. He sees what others do not and what he himself has never seen nor wanted to. So he closes his eyes as if to sleep. She is still resting her head on her hand, elbow on the table, and closes her eyes, too. Garby's ceases to be for the two of them and for the rest of the world. It is two in the morning. It is three, and he is talking.

"There were these four bored women, and one of them asked me for a drink, and then they all undressed. I went back every Saturday. The four of them for me, in all positions, through all the orifices. And the four of them also with each other, for me, for my eyes only."

She hears the immense pain behind so much pleasure. Unaware of it, she knows all about words.

It is half past three and he says, "I also came to see the sea."

"Then let's go," she says, and this is one of the few times she has opened her mouth. "There will be an icy wind, but it won't matter. If you came to see the sea, you've got to see it. You're not one of those people who does not do what they intend to."

She is somewhat dyslexic; at times she has written the word *mar* (sea) as *amr* (*amor*, love). So she knows that this is what he is trying to say, without meaning to.

They are walking on the long deserted jetty, whipped by the wind, and are compelled to hold each other so that they are not blown off. They hug and hug, walk a few steps, the bag dangling from his shoulders, and hold each other again. For him she is like a lifesaver; she accepts his embraces with some reservation, taking them as part of her new job, which has nothing, absolutely nothing to do with what people call emotions.

Careful, she warns herself, walking along this invisible yet outrageously loud sea; he is not a client, he is a patient, another desperate man, and I am not getting involved.

But he is also a client, and he invites her for a good sum of money to a hotel to spend what little is left of the night and maybe the following morning with each other. Just sleeping together, nothing else, he adds without kissing her.

That's better, much better, she thinks, the pay is good, and I don't see why not. Sleeping together can't be too exciting for him, better give him something for his money, and she rubs her hand over his chest and tries to get it inside his pants

Delicately, he removes her hand and says, "No, not now, maybe tonight and maybe not with you. Don't bother."

They do not go to the Imperial or any other four-star hotel. A client's whim, and what the heck. Although at some point at Garby's he had managed to arouse her feelings, their involvement had taken on now all the routine features – assuming false identities, signing in by other names, his bag still hanging from his shoulder just to give the situation a touch of credibility – and it is perhaps for the same reason that he books the room for two nights and pays in cash.

Once in the room she comes into action. She knows what to do on this score, but he does not welcome it. She gets angry, yet with some effort she gives free rein to her verbal routine. But her words are his words, those he had let loose at Garby's during the course of the night. She describes his scene: there he is having a drink with four women, not so young, women with experience. With each glassful, one after the other, they undress themselves in front of him. "It is hot, so hot in here," she moans with a kitten voice as each one of them would have done, undressing and giving him back his story with an unsuspected wealth of details.

He has taken his pants off, but she does not touch him. She is performing a strange dance, multiplying herself by four, and at the same time she is asking herself what he might be hiding in his bag, which is now hanging in the wardrobe. As if it mattered to her. He has locked the wardrobe and put the key away in his shirt pocket. He is now lying on the bed, still wearing his shirt like a coat of armor. She is carrying on her narrative. Suddenly he stops her. "Let me sleep," he says. "You can continue later. I like it, but I want to sleep now. I haven't slept for a long time. Let me sleep like this, curled up next to you. I have years of sleep to catch up with. Afterward, it will be different, you can go on telling me my story."

"Afterward, you will go with another woman, just as you said," she reminds him.

"Don't worry about what I said. I will pay you double rates. I want you here by my side, I really, really do, but let me sleep."

She knows that there are deeper needs, that sleeping is not the greatest at present, nor is lovemaking; yet he is already snoring lying by her side on the bed, modestly turning his back to her to face the wall.

In vain she tries to fall asleep. This man, I mean this client, intrigues her or, rather, irritates her. A reaction she can't allow herself; the client is a rat, all men are rats. After all, she is only there to earn her living, period. Without pondering unnecessarily any other kind of complications.

This man/client, on the other hand, seems to be having all sorts of complications and hidden intentions. What's that got to do with her? Perhaps the key to his problems is in his bag. Once paid, she can wash her hands of him and be off.

It must be very late, judging by her stomach. By his too. As he opens his eyes and looks at her he asks whether she would like to eat. She nods and he picks up the telephone and places an order. He must have gotten up before and consulted the menu; he does not consult her, yet she likes the sound of what he orders.

She goes to the bathroom, tidies herself up, and gets ready. Back in the room, he now has his pants on. After eating, he will no doubt go out looking for one or more women, more appetizing than she is, and she will be off the hook, as long as he pays what he has promised. He will go elsewhere with his bag and his perverse plans. Both amount to the same.

He had ordered wine, king crabs, and sirloin sandwiches. She receives the tray, and he picks up the bill. They eat, and eating is fun. He laughs for the first time. And she feels the need to open up and talk at length of things that have nothing to do with him but, rather, with her dreams.

"King crabs," she says. "I came to Comodoro because of this mythical delicacy; never tasted one before."

"Can't they be flown over?" he laughs.

"Yeah, but they are very expensive in Rosario. I'd heard about them, but I'd never been able to taste one."

"And did you like it when you did?"

"It was as if something had lit up inside me."

He stopped with his fork in the air waiting for her to finish her crab. And he waited to see her light up from inside, like the statuette of the Virgin he'd been given as a child, made of plaster and almost shapeless; not a graceful object in the daylight, but in the dark its phosphorescence shone in a wide range of colors. The barman at the airport had told him that this place lacked color, or something similar; yet this woman by his side, enjoying the last threads of crab meat and licking her lips, would suddenly sparkle with all the light and color in the world, and he, next to her, would forget the opacity of these last few years and radiate once again with happiness.

She had said that something had lit up inside her, and now he burst into laughter, a laughter that cries inside with so many tears because – he cannot nor does he want to explain it to her – because he realizes that he has reached the moment when metaphors seem to replace the literal truth, the virtual reality, while real life passes by. And this woman here, with her radiant smile but no inner light, as he had hoped, cannot save him. Ever.

After the laughter, she is now getting ready to go; to put an end to this farce, or rather to this interval between one farce and another. Leave this room, leave him to go and look for a young bird or the four mature tarts of his thirty-year-old dreams, while she sails off to spend her well-earned money. Before midnight so as to start the year 2000 with new shoes and even perhaps a new coat.

She puts out her hand to be paid, and he takes it and holds it.

"Don't go yet," he begs.

"Pay me what you like," she says. "It's seven o'clock, and it's time you prepared for your party. Today is already tomorrow, it is the eve of the future, the new year, the new century, the Antichrist, or whatever you wish to call it. You don't begin the year 2000 every day. . . . Make the best of it."

"I suppose you have a plan."

"I have no plan, and it doesn't matter. I'm happy. That it is so, I mean. All I have is time, and I don't want to waste yours."

"The same for me. All I have is time, and I don't want it. Stay with me. Talk to me. Let's have more crab. Champagne, if you like."

"This was not the arrangement."

"Look, I'll give you all I have, but stay and talk to me. It is a long time since . . ."

"It's a long time since anybody talked to you. I'm not staying, it does not interest me."

He went to the clothes rack, took the wallet from his coat. "Take it, take it all; it is a good deal more than the amount agreed. Stay."

"What about you?" she says in a more familiar tone, dropping her guard.

"It doesn't matter. That's what credit cards are for."

She turns back and sits on the bed. She unbuttons her blouse, in spite of the wind blowing outside, and lets her coat and bag fall on the floor. She's sad.

She closes her eyes not to see the silence. She has not touched his wallet.

He quietly moves near her and places a hand on the back of her head.

"The money is for you," he says softly as if he were talking of an intimate matter. "The money is all for you, it is more than you can imagine."

"I don't want to earn money like this, without having done my job, just listening."

"Many people do so, lawyers, analysts, doctors. Yes, even doctors."

"I'm a nurse," she says reluctantly, as if being a nurse were enough to justify her. "Well, in reality, I was a nurse in the past, but I am no longer."

"That's why I like you," he confesses, also with some reluctance, and acknowledging that, in spite of her age and her remote, almost harsh manners, he likes her.

"So," he adds, once more taking control of the situation, "we're going to have a siesta now and at ten tonight you wake me up to tell me again about the four women I was having a drink with. The time is ours, all ours. And I'm going to do to you and you are going to do to me . . . as never before. Don't forget to wake me up. I'll kill you, if you do."

She does not take his threat seriously, but she keeps a close eye on the watch. To relieve her boredom and not to feel like a silly romantic girl, she picks up his wallet and counts the money. There is certainly more than the sum arranged, but not that much more. So she starts to add it up. To kill time and not go on asking herself questions about the sleeper and building up false hopes, she makes a list of what she will buy with that money. Nothing practical, not on this millennium night. She won't pay the rent or get a new stove. Sheets yes, beautiful sheets, just for her in the boarding-house room where she'd never let a client come.

At ten o'clock on the dot she begins to wake him up gently, lying by his side and softly caressing his back: "Four beautiful, mature women are inviting you for a drink on Saturday evening," she reminds him, "and you go, although you are a married man, quite happily married."

This she guesses, for he has never told her so, not even insinuated it.

"Wait," he says, "don't move at all, just keep talking to me, just like this. So, I am thirty years old . . ."

Once in the bathroom, he locks himself in with his bag. She doesn't mind, she's not offended, nor does she feel he mistrusts her. She hears water running and after a long time he comes out; his hair is wet, but he's unshaven and still wearing the same underpants.

She says, "It's after eleven, and they will have already started celebrating. It won't be much of a party, but that's all we get here. It's an important moment. We could go to . . ."

"No, I'm planning a much better party," he says, and begins to undress her holding her by her hair. "We are going to make love as you have never made love in your life. You'll not be able to breathe for pleasure, little silly tart that you are; old bag, you're going to ask me for more, much more, but you won't be able to speak or breathe. And then all I'm asking is this: gather what little strength you have left after I've finished with you, fill the bathtub, and have the most luxurious bath of your life. I have left some foam there, of the best quality. Get inside that tub and stay there as long as necessary until you come out pure white and clean as you've never been. That's how I want to see you when you come back to this room. Stay a long time in that foam. I won't want you here for a while. And close the bathroom door well, lock it."

Eccentric requests like this do not worry her. So that's what he kept in his bag, a bottle of foam. He himself is pure foam. In the hospital they used a handful of sea salt and a tiny drop of ammonia, much more relaxing. But this man carries his own foam, is pure foam, and boasts like they all do: "You're going to burst with pleasure, bitch that you are, going to ask for more and more, you won't be able to move, you'll see how good it is, what a real man is, you're going to get the biggest prick in history, and things of the kind. If only. I am going to suck you up, I am going to . . ." How many times she's heard these promises. She's open to all proposals, why not? and could really like it, and on more than one occasion things really got steamy. But never as with the senior surgeon, very much the surgeon, and afterward, back to work. They're all the same. They all brag, but get scared shitless when a woman asks for her pleasure.

"I've condoms in my bag," she says, for in the middle of all his clamoring he seems to have forgotten such details.

"I don't use them."

"Condoms or nothing."

"You run no risks with me. It's years since . . . no risk."

She's seen the scar under his left breast, she knows of these things, and believes him.

"But you must not take any risks. Who can guarantee that I . . ." she says very sensibly.

"I don't care. Nothing matters to me, nothing."

He throws himself on top of her, and what before seemed asleep grows feathers and freely takes flight, just like this, without any manipulation or any effort on his behalf. They should call it "a bird," she thinks, joyful and full of expectations.

All that has been promised for centuries, from the beginning of the world, all that starts and ends and comes back and powerfully surges again is happening now. She rolls on golden sands, vibrates taut like a drum, tense as a rope; echoes the outcry of the spheres; opens and shuts, and the air enters in deep mouthfuls and makes her swell. She flies with that bird fluttering inside her and cries and cries with pleasure and happiness, for she knows that he is there flying with her, inside her, around her, and they are one, she and the other. A sudden purifying cascade, then an intimate beat, heavy and persistent.

She is resting now, sweating and satiated on top of him. With his remaining strength he moves her away and manages to whisper, "You promised me."

She knows: she'll go to the bathroom, fill the bath, and heap the foam in; it will be like a sea, which she can only reach with him at night. The foam will also caress her, entering all her crevices, but it will not be the same.

She stays for hours in the water, indulging in its warmth, in a sense of well-being long forgotten.

Then she dries in front of the mirror of the bathroom door and begins to see herself with new eyes. "I'm not so bad," she says to herself.

Her clothes are within her reach, and she begins slowly to dress herself, still looking and appreciating. That guy might want to go on sleeping until the following day, but not her. She wants to celebrate now more than ever. At Garby's the usual crowd will all be drunk, but they'll still go on having a great party throughout the night. Now that she has a little extra, she'll shout them all a glass of cider. He had said that they'd have champagne, but it doesn't matter, it's not worth hanging on for that. He has fulfilled his promise – and how – and she has kept hers. Given their age and circumstances, they both have good reasons to be satisfied. Where did he find so much verve, such boyish energy, she asks herself, as she finishes dressing. He seemed so apathetic, so unexcited, a bit of a slob, and suddenly, bang! Superman in bed. She dabs herself with the last drops of perfume left, thinking that, now, with a bit of luck, she will be able to buy a flacon of French essence.

In the half-lit room he seems to be still asleep on his back. She goes near to say "ciao," and perhaps "thank you," but after a few steps she notices the foam bubbling out of his mouth and understands. He is dead.

Her first instinct is to shake him, shout his name, perhaps give him artificial respiration or a cardiac massage. With great care she touches his forehead, and it feels very cold. It's too late to attempt resuscitation; besides, she is no longer a nurse, a good Samaritan, as perhaps she was at some stage in her life without meaning to. She's a cheap tart faced with a stiff and has to do something before

she gets into trouble. Poor chap. But this is not the time for com-
miserations. She goes back to the bathroom for a final check and,
of course, there is the empty blue pill box. A cure for erectile dys-
function, as they say. Now she understands his sudden passion.
She should have guessed. What an idiot, after his multiple bypass,
or whatever they fucking did to his heart. Goddamn son of a bitch,
she would like to shout at him, but better not make too much
noise, and think quickly; she doesn't want to complicate her life.

Fancy doing this to her. To come from so far away just to do this
to her. Little by little she puts things together, and she's furious.
She can go and leave him high and dry; return to the capital. After
all, he had paid for two days; she will hang the Do Not Disturb
sign on the door, take the first flight, and go somewhere else.
Somewhere new. Between her savings and what he paid her she
has some to spare. That's it, let him boil in his broth. She's off, and
he stays here to attract the flies, as he deserves. If only he had
looked for his four old sluts and had a drink with them, everything would have been fine. Although things did not go too badly
for him; he had what he wanted, and she'd done great honor to his
ejaculations.

And now all that's left is foam. Foam in his mouth. Even the
crummiest of detectives finding her there would charge her. She'd
better disappear altogether. Brazil, perhaps, or Venezuela: the farthest possible.

He must have some form of identification. Who is he? What do
I care? He must have more dough hidden away.

She knows what to do: it's cold outside, something that she ap-
preciates for the first time, and she has her gloves with her. She
puts them on to examine his pockets. She finds nothing; strange.
Just a pencil and some loose coins. No credit card, no documents,
no papers. But why be surprised, she asks herself. If she thinks
straight, why be surprised? He'd obviously planned it all in advance. Not to leave any trace. An anonymous suicide. Bloody hell!

And it had to happen to her. Aroused with so much passion, he could have died on top of her – and she trying to come with a stiff inside, to end the circle of her shitty existence.

Angrily, she turns to the bag he had left on the chair. No longer a question of respecting privacy with this poor man. But in the bag, surprise again: only two thick books, a notebook, a change of clothes, a pair of shoes, and a shaving knife.

A shaving knife, how strange, nobody uses them any more.

She places all these objects on a table, by the remains of their last meal. The books don't seem to mean anything. The notebook is unused. Pants, vests, socks, not new but clean, like the shoes. And the knife. She looks at it all for some time, not to look at the corpse, and suddenly she understands.

She is intelligent, that's it. She knows how to use the knife to carefully cut the inner lining of the bag, and there are the hundred-dollar bank notes, many more than she could have ever imagined, neatly stacked as interlining, one hundred and sixty of them. That is to say, sixteen thousand dollars, no mistake. She counts them all over again, makes little piles with them, little stacks of a thousand dollars. Whichever way it is, sixteen thousand smackers, and all for her.

Still in a counting mood she calculates; it is half past two in the morning, he's paid for two days, and we arrived twenty-four hours ago, which means I have until tomorrow midday. I must move fast, but there's no need to be frantic. The first flight to the capital leaves at 8:23. I have time before the cops hound me down. Here I am known as Silvia López, but not anywhere else. At 8:23 Silvia López vanishes. Round about midday they'll start calling for the room to be vacated and, when he doesn't answer, does not answer . . .

I shall be far away. I'm already on my way. I'm putting my coat on, packing the bundles of notes in its secret pockets – you can never take enough precautions with customers – but I would have never imagined that one could have such a sum of money, and my pockets are bursting, I must look like a kangaroo. No matter. On a night like this nothing matters. A new era begins today. For me more than for anybody else.

I'm off, happy in spite of the dead man. I'm off without thinking of him. I'll just whisper a gentle "ciao" from the door, "God bless you," which is all one can say in such ridiculous circumstances.

I'm taking not only your banknotes as souvenirs but also your knife and notebook.

January 1, 2000. Only four passengers are boarding this plane. None of them has a more honest face than I have. That's what you can expect on such a day.

She'd spent the remaining part of the night bundling up all her things, put a few clothes in a suitcase, adding the knife not to leave incriminating evidence, paid the rent, and said she was going to look after her sick sister. Nobody asks too many questions there, nobody cares. She didn't want to attract any attention, but all the same had to take a taxi on such a day. Now in the plane she's asking herself how on earth that slob of a man could have so much dough, from whom did he steal it. Let him be. It's now in very good hands. He must have known what kind of game he was playing, not with his money, but with his wretched pill. I'm going to become a duchess, she thinks, live in Angra dos Reis, where I always wanted to go, staying at the spa, enjoying all the foam baths in the world without anybody ordering me to. I'm going to travel all over Brazil, drink their famous *caipirinhas* the head nurse told us about, and she knew how to live. Or, rather, I'd better do my sums properly: with two hundred dollars a month, I can live perfectly well in a fishing village near Fortaleza, as that young resident doctor did, for years to come. I won't have to worry about a job; an honest one or a not so honest one, which had its points, while it lasted, and gave me this. I'll have enough for many, many a year. That's it. Fantastic. At the airport I'll take the first flight to Uruguay and, if there is no flight, I'll go by hovercraft, and from there straight to lovely old Brazil, to find myself a suitable little village. By the time they try in vain to wake up that poor slob, I'll be abroad.

Not just intelligent, I'm brilliant. And today I was lucky.

Or so she thinks.

Why did she then keep the blank notebook of that "poor slob" as she refers to the dead man?

We see her now flying to Buenos Aires at an altitude of twenty-six thousand feet, writing feverishly something that looks like a letter. We see her now going to the toilet with her coat on, in spite of the heating system being on full blast.

Now we do not see her, nor do we care.

Epilogue

At six in the evening on the first of January in Comodoro Rivadavia, Garby's is closed, hermetically sealed. Yet streaks of light – an indication of life – leak from inside, and somebody's furiously beating at the windows, one after the other, with unusual urgency. Asleep on top or under the tables, people jump up and call to the barman to go and see what the hell is going on. Exhausted and still half sozzled, the barman shuffles to the door to confront a well-endowed woman, though he has not enough energy to welcome her properly. "What? . . ." he begins to ask, but she quickly drops a package in his hands as if it scolded her.

"You are the barman, aren't you? Yes, I recognize you. This package was given to me by a passenger this morning who made me swear by my mother and all I hold sacred to let you have it this same day. The return flight was delayed, but here I am. I am an airhostess and have done my duty."

The barman feels obliged to pull himself together, sober up, have a triple espresso, put all the lights on, and read the letter. For when he opened the plastic package badly held together with tape and strings, brand new hundred-dollar notes fell out of it. Surely the hour had come to clear out his alcoholic fumes.

The letter starts by saying, "My darling barman, you are the only person I can trust. You saw how we two met a couple of nights ago."

Here follows a long saga about the nights of December 30 and 31 of the last century, last millennium, about a meeting and a death that, in reality, was a strange form of suicide.

At the end the letter says, "I left the dead man in the hotel. I don't know who he is. We gave false names – in Comodoro I always do. Please understand. All I know is that I want him to have a Christian burial. And in case they don't find his relatives (police and lawyers are so inefficient) and even if they find them, here are six thousand dollars for the funeral. With all the pomp and glory the dead man deserves. And don't you dare keep the money for yourself – as I am not – for if you do, I'll make sure that all the curses of this world, and a little extra more, fall on your head."

The bottom of the letter is wet, as if soaked with tears; you can hardly read the signature.

"What the hell," grumbles Garby's barman. "Romantic messages should never be wrapped up in plastic; they get all blurred."

Translated from the Spanish by Psiche Hughes

Andrea Blanqué, "Inmensamente Eunice," in *Esas malditas mujeres: Antología de cuentistas latinoamericanas,* ed. Angélica Gorodischer (Buenos Aires: Ameghino, 1998), 131–41.

Marilyn Bobes, "En Florencia, diez años después," in *Alguien tiene que llorar* (Buenos Aires: Ameghino, 1998), 113–23.

Carmen Boullosa, "An Impossible Story," chapter 17 of *Llanto: Novelas imposibles* (Mexico City: Era, 1992), 100–105.

Fanny Buitrago, "El mar en la ventana," in *Líbranos de todo mal* (Bogotá: Carlos Valencia, 1989), 29–34.

Margo Glantz, "English Love," in *Zona de derrumbe* (Rosario, Argentina: Beatriz Viterbo, 2001), 93–102.

Liliana Heker, "Cuando todo brille," in *Las peras del mal* (Buenos Aires: Belgrano, 1982), 9–19.

Sylvia Lago, "Días dorados de la Señora Pieldediamantes," in *Detrás de la reja: Antología crítica de narradoras latinoamericanas del siglo XX,* ed. Celia Correas de Zapata (Caracas: Monte Ávila, 1980), 352–74.

Ángeles Mastretta, "Aunt Mariana," in *Women with Big Eyes (Mujeres de ojos grandes),* trans. Amy Schildhouse Greenberg, copyright © 2003 by Ángeles Mastretta. Used by permission of Riverhead Books, an imprint of Penguin Group (USA), Inc.

Nélida Piñon, "Cortejo do divino," in *Sala de armas* (Rio de Janeiro: Sabiá, 1973), 64–71.

Elena Poniatowska, "Love Story," in *De noche vienes* (Mexico City: Grijalbo, 1979), 83–92.

Teresa Ruiz Rosas, "Detrás de la calle Toledo," in *El cuento peruano, 1990–2000,* ed. Ricardo González Vigil (Lima: Cope, 2001), 607–21.

Cristina Peri Rossi, "La destrucción o el amor," in *Los pecados capitales,* ed. Lourdes Ortiz (Barcelona: Grijalbo, 1990), 57–64.

Source Acknowledgments

Ana María Shua, "La despedida," in *Los amores de Laurita* (Buenos Aires: Sudamericana, 1984), 151–61.

Armonía Somers, "El derrumbamiento," in *Todos los cuentos*, 1953–1967 (Montevideo: Arca, 1967), 9–22.

Alicia Steimberg, "Young Amatista," in *Amatista* (Barcelona: Tusquets, 1989), 108–13, 115–20, 34–38.

Luisa Valenzuela, "Fin de milenio," in *Cuentos completos y uno más* (Buenos Aires: Alfaguara, 1999), 555–74.

ANDREA BLANQUÉ, born in Montevideo, is collaborator of *El País Cultural*, the Uruguayan supplement of *El País*. She has edited anthologies of short stories and published books of poetry, including *Canción de cuna para un asesino* (1992) and *El cielo sobre Montevideo* (1997), and the books of stories *No fueron felices* (1990) and *Querida muerte* (1993). The story included here was only published in the anthology *Esas malditas mujeres* (1998).

MARILYN BOBES, born in Havana, has worked as a journalist at *La Prensa Latina* and is vice president of the Unión de Escritores y Artistas de Cuba. She has published books of poetry, including *La aguja en el pajar* (1979) and *Hallar el modo* (1989), and is considered one of the most talented contemporary writers. Her book of stories entitled *Alguien tiene que llorar* (1950) won the Premio Casa de las Américas. Much of her work has been translated in the United States and in European countries.

CARMEN BOULLOSA, born in Mexico City, has published many novels, including *Antes* (1989), *Llanto* (1992), *Duerme* (1994), *Cielos de la tierra* (1997), and *Treinta años* (1999). Her novel *La milagrosa* (1994), which has been translated into English, won the Frankfurt Literature Prize in 1996. She has lectured widely in the United States, held the Latin American chair for January 2001 at the Sorbonne, and has since been in residence as a visiting scholar at the New York Public Library and at New York University. She has written several plays for her theater in Coyoacán (Mexico City) and a collection of poems entitled *La Delirios* (1998).

FANNY BUITRAGO, born in Baranquilla, Colombia, has written many novels, including *Cola de zorro* (1970), *Los pañamanes* (1979), and *Los amores de Afrodita* (1983), and collections of short stories: *La otra gente* (1973), *Bahía Sonora* (1975), and *¡Líbranos de todo mal!* (1989). She is also the author of such works of children's literature as *Cantos del palomar* (1988) and *La casa del verde doncel* (1990).

MARGO GLANTZ, born in Mexico City, has worked as a journalist and as an academic. She is the author of more than twenty works of fiction and literary criticism, some of which have been awarded literary prizes. She is famous for her anthology of young Mexican writers entitled *Onda y escritura en México* (1971) and her book on Sor Juana Inés de la Cruz (1996). She has also published such erotic texts as *Apariciones* (1996) and *Zona de derrumbe* (2001). *Las genealogías* (1996), a book affectionately telling her family history, has been translated into English as *The Family Tree* (1997).

LILIANA HEKER, born in Buenos Aires, is the author of several collections of short stories, *Los que vieron la zarza* (1966), *Un resplandor que se apagó en el mundo* (1978), and *Las peras del mal* (1982). Other works include *Bordes de lo real* (1991), *Fin de historia* (1996), *Zona de clivaje* (1997), inspired by Virginia Woolf's creation, *Shakespeare's Sister*. A constant theme in her work is the dark side of everyday life, which often invokes the absurd and the mad.

SYLVIA LAGO, born in Montevideo, took part in the Latin American feminist movement in the 1960s. She has published several novels, including *Trájanos* (1962), *Tan solos en el balneario* (1963), and *El corazón de la noche* (1987), and such short-story collections as *Detrás del rojo* (1967), *La última razón* (1968), *Los últimos cuentos* (1972), and *Días dorados y días en sombra* (1996). Her fiction is often marked by the satirical denunciation of the hypocrisy of sexual conventions.

ANGELES MASTRETTA, born in Puebla (Mexico), established her reputation as a writer with her first novel, *Arráncame la vida* (1985), which won the Premio Mazatlán. Her first collection of short stories, *Mujeres de ojos grandes* (1990), which received great acclaim in Mexico and abroad, has been translated into five languages. It was followed by another collection, *Puerto libre*, in 1994, and by a novel, *Mal de amores* (1995).

NÉLIDA PIÑON, born in Rio de Janeiro, started her writing career as a journalist and published her first novel, *Guia mapa de Gabriel Arcanjo*, in 1961. Other novels include *A casa de paixão* (1972), in which she argues the case for women expressing their sexuality, *A força do destino* (1977), and the allegorical work *A doce canção de Caetana* (1987). Other novels include *A Républica dos sonhos* (1984), which has been translated into English. She has published a number of short-story collections, such as *Tempo das frutas* (1966) and *Sala de armas* (1973).

ELENA PONIATOWSKA, born in Mexico City, was deeply involved in Mexican politics and in 1971 wrote a renowned report on the massacre of demonstrating students by the military, *La noche de Tlatetoco* (1971). Her novel *Hasta no verte Jesús mio* (1969) has been translated into English, as have some of her uncollected short stories. She has published collections of short stories, including *De noche vienes* (1979). More recent work includes *Querido Diego, te abraza Quiela* (1978), which is centered on the life and marriage of Diego Rivera, *La flor de lis* (1988), and *Tinísima* (1992), a fictionalized biography of the Italian American photographer Tina Modotti.

CRISTINA PERI ROSSI, born in Montevideo, has lived in exile in Spain since 1972, after publishing her first novel, *El libro de mis primos* (1969), her first collection of short stories, *Los museos abandonados* (1968), and her first poems, *Evohé* (1971), in Uruguay. She has continued to write in all genres – including the novels *Una pasión prohibida* (1986) and *Solitario de amor* (1988) and the verse collections *Cosmogonía* (1988) and *Babel Bárbara* (1991) – and has recently published another short-story collection, *Desastres íntimos* (1997). Much of her work has been translated into English, including my translation of her novel *La nave de los locos* (1984) as *The Ship of Fools* (1989).

TERESA RUIZ ROSAS, born in Arequipa, is one of the most interesting voices of contemporary Peruvian narrative. Her writing often focuses on unveiling the deepest – sometimes pathological – motivations of the human psyche. Among her work figure a collection of stories, *El desván* (1990), and the novel *El copista* (1994). The short story that appears in this collection won the Juan Rulfo Prize at the Cervantes Institute in Paris in 1999.

Contributors

ANA MARÍA SHUA, born in Buenos Aires, is the author of novels and collections of short stories, many of which have been translated and published in Italy, Germany, and the United States; and of children's books, for which she has won several prizes. She established her reputation in 1980 with her novel *Soy paciente* (1980), and won a Guggenheim scholarship for her novel *El libro de los recuerdos*. (1994). This was followed in 1997 by *La muerte como efecto secundario*. Her latest collection of stories, *Como una buena madre*, was published in 2001. The story included in this collection is taken from *Los amores de Laurita* (1984), which was made into a film.

ARMONÍA SOMERS was born in Montevideo. Her first novel, *La mujer desnuda* (1950), made her reputation as an avant-garde writer and one of the first Latin American feminists. This novel was followed by a vast amount of other fiction, such as the novels *De medio en medio* (1965), *Un retrato para Dickens* (1969), and *Sólo los elefantes encuentran mandrágora* (1986). Her short stories have been collected under the title *Todos los cuentos* (1967).

ALICIA STEIMBERG, born in Buenos Aires, is the author of many novels, such as *Músicos y relojeros* (1971), *La loca 101* (1973), *El árbol del placer* (1986), *Amatista* (1989), and *Cuando digo Magdalena* (1992), as well as short stories, *Como todas las mañanas* (1983). In all her work, eroticism combines with striking surrealistic imagery.

LUISA VALENZUELA was born in Buenos Aires. Her novels *Hay que sonreír* (1966) and *El gato eficaz* (1972) made her name as one of the most original writers of her generation. Her two political satires, *Cola de lagartija* (1983) and *Realidad nacional desde la cama* (1990), have been translated into English, as have some stories from her short-story collections: *Aquí pasan cosas raras* (1975), *Cambio de armas* (1982), *Donde viven las águilas* (1983), *Simetrías* (1993), *Cuentos completos y uno más* (1998), and *Los deseos oscuros y los otros* (2002).

In the *Latin American Women Writers* series

Underground River and Other Stories
By Inés Arredondo
Translated by Cynthia Steele
With a foreword by Elena Poniatowska

Dreams of the Abandoned Seducer: Vaudeville Novel
By Alicia Borinsky
Translated by Cola Franzen in collaboration with the author
With an interview by Julio Ortega

Mean Woman
By Alicia Borinsky
Translated and with an introduction by Cola Franzen

The Fourth World
By Diamela Eltit
Translated and with a foreword by Dick Gerdes

The Women of Tijucopapo
By Marilene Felinto
Translated and with an afterword by Irene Matthews

The Youngest Doll
By Rosario Ferré

Industrial Park: A Proletarian Novel
By Patrícia Galvão (Pagu)
Translated by Elizabeth Jackson and K. David Jackson

Violations: Stories of Love by Latin American Women
Edited and with and introduction by Psiche Hughes

In a State of Memory
By Tununa Mercado
Translated by Peter Kahn
With an introduction by Jean Franco

Call Me Magdalena
By Alicia Steimberg
Translated by Andrea G. Labinger